TOBI LAKMAKER was born in 1994 and lives in Amsterdam.
He writes columns for *De Volkskrant*. *The History of My Sexuality* is his first book.

KRISTEN GEHRMAN has translated the work of Dola de Jong
and Lize Spit, among others.

The History of My Sexuality

Tobi Lakmaker

Translated from the Dutch by
Kristen Gehrman

GRANTA

Granta Publications, 12 Addison Avenue, London W11 4QR

First published in Great Britain by Granta Books, 2024
This paperback edition published by Granta Books, 2025

Originally published in the Netherlands in 2021 as
De geschiedenis van mijn seksualiteit by Das Mag Uitgeverij B.V.

Lines from *Polleke* by Guus Kuijer (Querido, 2009), translated into
English by Kristen Gehrman, reproduced by permission of Querido.
Lines from *Catcher in the Rye* by J. D. Salinger (Penguin, 2019)
reproduced by permission of Penguin Random House UK.

The publisher gratefully acknowledges the support
of the Dutch Foundation for Literature.

N ederlands
letterenfonds
dutch foundation
for literature

A CIP catalogue record for this book
is available from the British Library

1 3 5 7 9 10 8 6 4 2

ISBN 978 1 78378 883 5
eISBN 978 1 78378 882 8

Typeset by Iram Allam in Garamond
Printed and bound by CPI Group (UK) Ltd, Croydon, CR0 4YY
www.granta.com

PROLOGUE

My Mother is a Patrilineal Jew

My mother always said, 'Our friends aren't rich, they just bought a house at the right time.' My parents bought a house at exactly the right time – on Jacob Obrechtstraat, number seven, right in the middle of Oud-Zuid. Somebody once said that there are two types of people who live in Amsterdam's Oud-Zuid: the nouveau riche and intellectual Jews. We weren't nouveau riche, as far as I was led to believe, and we weren't technically Jewish – my mother is a *patrilineal* Jew – and when I asked my father what an intellectual was, he replied, 'The only true intellectual is Wilfred Oranje.'

When I was twenty, I actually rented the same room that Wilfred Oranje had lived in – he was dead by then, but all the books he translated were still there. I woke up every morning surrounded by the works of Sigmund Freud. I didn't last there very long. I wanted to be an intellectual too, but every time I tried to read a book I fell asleep. That's just how it is with me – if I stare too long at any work by a man who looks like Sigmund Freud, I fall asleep.

Between the ages of eighteen and twenty-two, I tried to absorb all kinds of Sigmund Freuds, and in the end I was left with only one clearly describable feeling: I wasn't Sigmund Freud. Or more specifically – I wasn't a man, I was a woman. And I had a *really* hard time being a woman. They wanted me to grow my hair long. Of course, nobody ever said it out loud, but when people want to shove something down your throat, they don't need words. They just make sure you *know*.

Nowadays, my hair is really short, and I'm in a support group for transgender people. You want to know more about that? Just call me. Oh, I'm not transgender by the way – I'm just a person who enjoys penetrating women and is tired of having to buy *devices* to do it. They cost a fortune, and half the time you don't know what you're doing because the ridiculously expensive gadget's gone crooked. You know what I'm fed up with? Things being crooked.

I know, I could've started reading books by people who don't look like Sigmund Freud – women, for example, or men of colour. Or better still – women of colour. But the point is that those books aren't part of the *canon*. The fucking canon. Now I hear you thinking – Woolf is part of the canon, Baldwin is part of the canon. But I'll be straight with you – I haven't actually read James Baldwin yet and Virginia Woolf puts me to sleep too. As soon as she said that she would buy those flowers herself, I was out cold.

When I was about seventeen, I decided I wanted to be a

genius. The annoying thing about being a genius is that it's like being a homosexual: you don't *become* one, you just turn out to be one. At least, that's what they say. If you ask me, geniuses are just ordinary people who managed not to pick up the phone every time the world wanted something from them and instead focused their energy on something the world didn't know it was waiting for. That said, there were a lot of times *I* didn't answer my phone either, so many in fact that my friends eventually just gave up. They started talking about me behind my back and concluded that there must be something wrong with me, that they could tell by the way I looked at Zahra that I was *definitely* a lesbian. Right they were – on all fronts.

After the girls dumped me, I started hanging out with Felix and Chiel more often. Of all the kids at our very white, very exclusive high school, they were the whitest and the most exclusive of them all, and I guess I liked that. During the break, Chiel pretty much said just one thing, 'Oh, is *that* all?' and Felix would nod. I nodded too, but I never knew exactly what he was talking about. I only knew that he was right, because white exclusive people were always right. I was almost never right, and that's something that got harder for me over time.

In fact, I was pretty much wrong about everything. Wrong about boys and wrong about girls, wrong about the right answers and, more importantly, wrong about the right questions. A person can have all the answers they want, but if they don't ask the right questions, those answers will always be speaking into the void. *That's* what I figured out. I figured out that there are answers that precede questions. And as long as those answers are wrong, that's all you'll ever be – wrong.

I

THE
HISTORY
OF MY
SEXUALITY

Walter the Recruitment Consultant

The history of my sexuality is that I have always been looking for someone to close all the doors and windows, someone who would say, okay, that's enough now. More precisely, first I was into men and later into women, but really always into women; into Muriel, my long-legged, red-headed tutor – into so many women really – but I kept my eyes and something else extremely crucial closed. Not that any of that is actually relevant.

I lost my virginity to Walter the Recruitment Consultant, but that's something I'd rather not dwell on. He voted conservative, and when I was really struggling to get excited, I tried to focus on that, to channel that weird connection between horniness and hate.

I lost my virginity on Sarphatistraat in a house on the Weesperplein with a long flagpole jutting out of the facade. I always recognize it by the flagpole. It reminds me of Walter's chubby, demanding erection. Walter was very sweet. The night it happened he said, 'I think I'm more nervous than you are.' And he *was* more nervous than me. To be honest, I couldn't have cared less.

The reason I wanted to lose my virginity was that I wanted to be PD-ed, or 'properly deflowered'. Milan and I were spending a lot of time at Coffee Company when we were supposed to be in class, and we talked about being PD-ed constantly. Or more specifically, we talked about the period of reckless debauchery that would inevitably follow being PD-ed. Being PD-ed was a euphemism we had invented for our future children, who would undoubtedly come to us one day and ask: 'Who was the first person you ever slept with?' And we'd be ready with a very chaste answer.

Milan eventually lost his virginity in a toilet at the VU Medical Center – he went on to study medicine. I lost mine to Walter on the night of 1 September 2011. After that, we continued to see each other for a while, not because I enjoyed being with him, but because it was necessary for keeping up appearances. Walter and I met at Café Mazzeltof, right after I'd texted the TV presenter Matthijs van Nieuwkerk. He was the guy I actually wanted to sleep with, but he never texted back. I got his number from my brother, because he had a lot of connections. That's what I craved at seventeen: sex and a lot of connections.

I'd ducked into a snack bar round the corner so I could

fully concentrate on my message to Van Nieuwkerk. When I got back to the Mazzeltof I saw Walter standing there and immediately planted a kiss on his cheek. Betsie was sitting at the back of the bar. I walked up to her and said, 'This is the one.' Since the day I'd met her, Betsie had always been a bit prettier than me, which made going out with her a nightmare. I was always the second choice. So it was up to me to make sure the guys believed that there was really only one option – me, Sofie Lakmaker.

To keep Betsie out of Walter's sight, I offered to get us another round. At the bar, I tried to make eye contact with him. He looked incredibly nervous, so in an effort to reassure him, I passed him the beer I'd bought for Betsie. 'You know, we could be making out right now,' I said. 'I don't like assertive women,' he replied. I nodded, then we started making out.

A week later, we met at another bar, the Lempicka. He told me he was from the South and his grandfather was the guy who figured out that you could make biodiesel out of old frying oil, which is why his parents now had a swimming pool in the backyard. I told him I wanted to study philosophy after high school. He responded by saying I must be a liberal. To which I said he must be a conservative, and then I suggested we go back to his place.

We made out on the bed for a long time, and after fifteen minutes I said, 'Let's just do it.' Walter was terrified. I was too, actually, but I had no time to lose – or so I thought. He was twenty-six and I was seventeen, and that's the crazy thing: the more time you have, the more rushed you feel. I remember how his boxers were already a little too tight, and how they got even tighter with his half-stiff dick in them. Later it turned out that Walter was only ever half-stiff. He had to tug at himself to keep it up. One time he wanted me to do it for him, but apparently I jerked way too hard.

My girlfriends were all disappointed by their first time. 'Was that *it*?' they all said. I thought it was wild. Maybe not in an entirely good way. More like a plane crash is wild – overwhelming, like you're not sure you'll ever be able to explain what happened. Walter's dick was all over the place. After a while, he said, 'I want you to kiss it.' Honestly, I thought it was ludicrous, but I did it anyway. If you never do things you think are ludicrous, you'll never get anywhere in life.

After Walter came, he said, 'Will you promise me that we'll never do it like this again?' He was referring to the fact that we hadn't used a condom. I can't remember why we didn't – it's not like we were caught up in the heat of the moment. The whole thing took hours. I used to tell people that I lost my virginity to 'Everywhere' by Fleetwood Mac, and it's true that the song did play at some point, but really, I lost my virginity to the entire history of Western pop.

When I woke up, Patrick was standing in the doorway. Patrick was Walter's housemate, and to be honest, I found him significantly more attractive than Walter. He had slick, combed-back hair, and though he, too, was from the South, he pronounced his 'g's a little less softly than you might have expected. To put it bluntly, Patrick looked like a prick, but I liked that about him. At least he was something. Walter looked more like somebody standing next to you on the subway who you'd eventually have to ask to step out of the way. I swear, that's really what Walter looked like.

Patrick was searching around for his tie, and when I turned over to ask Walter if he knew where it was, I saw that the bed was empty. He had already left for work – he did something in *recruitment*. Don't ask me what exactly this job entailed; all I know is that he made shitloads of money doing it. He was employed by the municipality of Utrecht, which I found fairly depressing. Maybe that was my biggest fear: to be *employed*. Especially by the municipality of Utrecht.

Patrick worked for a start-up in Amsterdam, and when he realized that Walter had already left, he grinned at me. He asked if the two of us had had a *nice* time together. I replied that we'd had a terribly nice time together, which seemed to surprise him. People don't exactly love it when you use words like 'terribly' all the time. Maybe it's another way of sounding too assertive.

Patrick stood there in the doorway for another fifteen minutes, which made me uneasy. I had absolutely no clothes on, and I'm pretty sure he knew that. Talking while naked to someone who is fully dressed, except for the tie, definitely affects the dynamic. Finally, I said, 'Okay, I'm going to read *Quote 500* now.' The magazine was lying next to Walter's bed along with a couple of books that explained how to make insane amounts of money with relatively little effort. Just convert some old frying oil into biodiesel, I'd have said, but apparently it's more complicated than that.

Not long after I'd lost my virginity, Patrick and Walter moved into a house in Zeeburg. They bought it from the newly elected mayor, Eberhard van der Laan, who had moved into his official residence. He left behind a pretty nice piece of property. It was decorated by Patrick's latest fuck buddy, Lianne, who had godawful taste. Lianne was a dental assistant, and it showed in her furniture choices. Everything about that house in Zeeburg gave you the feeling that your teeth were about to be ripped out of your mouth.

And as if Lianne's assault on the interior wasn't bad enough, there was Patrick. He made sure to leave books by Ray Kluun lying all over the house. I swear, everywhere you looked, your eyes would land on one of those nauseating titles. 'A great guy,' Patrick would say. It drove me insane. Still, Patrick was more interesting to talk to than Walter, who I was barely talking to at all by then. He was always trying to get me to read books about exploring my own body, but I really wasn't into that. Which is why I usually ended up talking to Patrick and Lianne over breakfast and during all the other downtime. At least with them there was something to experience, you know? Lianne was very religious, and Patrick was always saying 'goddamn' just to piss her off. Then he'd look at me with a twinkle in his eye, and we'd both laugh. Great guy, that Patrick.

On 22 November 2011, Walter posted on Facebook that he was single and looking for a relationship. Furious, I called him up, and he immediately answered the phone even though he was driving. He had one of those hands-free devices. 'Aw baby, you're *seventeen*,' he said. 'Oh, right,' I replied. For a second, all I could hear was the rumbling on the highway, and then he whispered, 'If you were twenty-three, I would've already asked you to marry me.' Even that sounded ludicrous, and there are days when I wonder what would have happened if we had got married. I'd probably have been employed somewhere, and maybe that wouldn't have been so bad.

Call it Love

In 2018, someone wrote a very bad book about me entitled *Call it Love*. A ridiculous title, of course. Personally, I would've given it the title *Call it Love, or Something Like it*, because what we had only remotely resembled love. In the book, my character's name is 'Girl A', which is pretty stupid when you think about it. I have a name, it's Sofie Lakmaker. And no, I haven't actually read the book, only the reviews, and they were pretty damning. That was enough for me. Some say that critics are just normal people, but not me. As far as I'm concerned, critics are always right, which means they satisfy a lifelong need of mine: being right.

On the cover is a picture of a super-pretty girl, way prettier than I am – or was back when I was dating Douchebag D – that's what I call him. He probably caught on to this after a while, but he didn't have a chance to make things right, because the critics made sure his book never saw a second edition.

My mum always said that revenge is a dish best served cold, but I'm not sure whether I'm actually out for revenge. Maybe the critics have already taken revenge for me, maybe revenge doesn't matter. Revenge is for people who feel rancour – I mostly just feel hurt.

I met Douchebag D when I was four and he was twelve – obviously this wasn't the start of our relationship. He and my brother Daniel were best friends, and for some reason he never wanted to play at our house, only at his. My parents immediately distrusted him for that, but not me. I've never been a suspicious type. Let alone when I was four.

We saw each other for the first time in years at Daniel's twenty-sixth birthday party. I had just lost my virginity to Walter the Recruitment Consultant, and I told him about it in great detail. While I was talking, I noticed a burning interest in his eyes, a look that I think you could translate as 'Behold, a woman who speaks.'

Afterwards we cycled home together, and I really needed to pee. So I squatted on the street, and again he gave me that look: 'Behold, a woman who pees.' I must have come as a true revelation to Douchebag D. A few months later he messaged me to ask how I did on my final exams. I replied that I averaged 7.8, technically 8.3 if you only counted the central written exam.

To celebrate, we met up for a drink at Café de Wetering, where I asked him if he was satisfied with his penis. He replied that he hadn't received too many complaints. Then he asked me once again what I wanted to do with my life, because who *doesn't* ask you that when you're eighteen, and I don't really remember what I said. I'm pretty sure I didn't respond and then proceeded to tell him that my mum had cancer. 'That sucks,' he said.

When Café de Wetering closed, we went to Café De Spuyt. It was a pretty tacky bar, and a few hours later we went to an even tackier one – the Mazzeltof. I couldn't have cared less if we ran into Walter. Actually, I was hoping Lianne and Patrick would be there. I wanted to ask Patrick if he still thought Kluun was such a great guy. But he wasn't there and nor was Lianne.

The nice thing about Walter was that I could be with him without having to concentrate on him at all. Douchebag D, on the other hand, was forever asking questions. Finally, I asked him a question: 'Do you think Daniel would mind?' He gave me a thoughtful look and said something about girls growing up to be women. It got pretty exhausting after a while – all of his revelations about girls and women, and the exact moment they transitioned from one to the other.

I'm pretty sure Daniel hated it. A few weeks later, I was sitting with him at a bar, and I said, 'Okay, we should talk about Douchebag D.' 'No,' he replied. The crazy thing about Daniel is that when he says stop, you stop. At least I do, anyway. Then he said that he thought I should move to Prague for a little while. And Daniel being Daniel, I actually considered it.

Anyway, after Mazzeltof, Douchebag D and I wandered the

streets for a while. It was pretty obvious that we both wanted to kiss each other, but we didn't dare. At the corner of the Ruysdaelkade, I said, 'Come on, son.' And we kissed. The sun was just beginning to rise, and life was breathing with possibilities; if you asked me, I'd have said I was nothing without perfectly straightened hair. I did all those things with Walter too, but he was always in such a hurry – he had to get back to the municipality of Utrecht. Douchebag D and I, on the other hand, were almost always together, and that got pretty unbearable. It's hard to explain, but after a while, you just can't breathe any more. If you're *sometimes* pretty for long enough, you'll eventually suffocate. Take it from me.

Another product of the week when I got fired from Bagels & Beans was a poem about my perineum. *To* my perineum, actually. It was a letter of apology for constantly exposing it to the result of such insincere pleasure. Sex with Douchebag D was, in a word, awful. Really awful. I don't even know where to begin – or whether I should begin. In any case, it was always the same: we'd sit on the couch at his place, and then we'd get to kissing. Somewhat passionately, somewhat indifferently. Then he'd stand up – which I hated, I never wanted him to stand up – and we'd walk to his bedroom. Then we'd lie on the bed, me underneath, him on top.

I'm not sure how much detail I need to go into at this point. Basically, the whole thing led to the same monotonous ritual – me making the same noises, him making the same facial expressions. Afterwards, he'd walk out of the room and disappear for about ten minutes. I never knew what was going on during those ten minutes. When he came back, he'd throw a towel at me. It always made me feel like a whore. But mostly I was relieved that our little routine was over again.

Nowadays, I have friends who say, 'But *Sof*, hetero sex just sucks like that.' But I don't believe that. There must be people who enjoy it. I guess I'm just not one of them.

A few months after our kiss on the Ruysdaelkade, Douchebag D and I took off to the Lido for a long weekend. The Lido is a seaside resort near Venice. According to Wikipedia, it formed the backdrop for Thomas Mann's novel *Death in Venice*. I haven't read it, but after that trip, I probably could've written it myself. Something in me died that weekend. Exactly what, I can't tell you, but it had something to do with my belief in a happy ending. For me and Douchebag D, but more importantly for me and my existence as a muse.

Oh god, the muses. I met one that weekend, and what a muse she was. She was the wife of An Awfully Famous Author, and I'd like to mention her by name but I don't remember what it was. Maybe she never told me. Knowing her, she probably introduced herself as 'the wife of An Awfully Famous Author'.

Douchebag D was there to interview her husband for *Vrij Nederland*. He was a man who already enjoyed a glorious reputation as a great European writer, but since the EU was once again under a lot of pressure, people seemed to think it would be a good idea for him to get even more recognition. However, he had another reputation too – for being a Dirty Bastard. And if there's one group that's under pressure these days, it's *them* – the Dirty Bastards of the world.

The evening after the interview, the four o[...]
dinner: me, Douchebag D, the Creep and his w[...]
thing the Creep said to me was that I was probably eve[...]
with my hair down, which he was right about. But I'd forg[...]
to bring my hair straightener to the Lido, so I had no choi[...]
but to wear it up. After that little comment, he started making
all kinds of lofty statements on the Human Condition, about
which I had plenty of opinions myself, but every word that came
out of his mouth was exclusively directed at Douchebag D.

So eventually I was stuck talking to the Creep's wife, which
I found fairly exhausting. We discovered that she had worked
for the Rijksmuseum, where my father had also worked, and
I was hoping that she'd at least be able to tell me what he
actually did there, because nobody really knew. My dad never
said a word about his job. My mother always said, 'Your father
might as well work for the Secret Service.' Every once in a
while, he would say something, but it was the kind of statement that made you even more confused. 'The Pig was at it
again today' – *that* was the kind of thing he'd say.

The Pig was my dad's boss, and she and my father didn't
see eye to eye. I met her once, at Museum Night. She handed
me a stick with some strawberries on it and told me I could
dip it in the chocolate fountain if I wanted to. Then my father
said I could also look at some paintings, since we were in a
museum after all. And I did look at the paintings for a little
while, but I kept sneaking back to the fountain. It revealed
a certain sense of foresight in the Pig: people like chocolate
more than they like art.

in the end, she lasted longer at the Rijksmuseum than my dad did. The Pig survived the Great Shift, and my father did not. The Great Shift was a time when all the employees who preferred museums to chocolate shops got fired. My father had the wrong *mindset*, so they gave him a silver handshake. We went on a lot of vacations with that money, and as I explained all this to the Creep's wife, she just kept saying, 'Oh he wouldn't remember me.' I'm telling you, comments like that drive me insane.

An hour later we left for a restaurant chosen by the Creep. We had to take a ferry to get there, and it was on that ferry that he started pinching my calves. I was shocked, and I think Douchebag D was too, but he had this weird smile plastered on his face. I think that smile was supposed to say, 'He's awfully famous, just give him a little feel.'

I thought otherwise. I asked the Creep what the hell he was doing, and his lips curled into a smile. 'I heard you're planning to cycle across Europe,' he said, which was true, I was. I was happier on my bike than anywhere else, so I thought, why not just stay on the bike? I nodded, and the Creep mumbled, 'Just checking if you're ready.'

At the table, things got a bit awkward because the Creep kept trying to put the moves on the waitress. I didn't blame him – she was a beautiful girl. But actually it was even worse when she wasn't there – then he'd ignore his wife completely, talk only to Douchebag D and occasionally remark that I should finish my calamari.

But I couldn't take it any more. I'd ordered a pizza as an

appetizer, and by then I was so full that I could've lived off tangerines for the rest of my life. Out of the corner of my eye, I could tell that the Creep's wife was on my side. When he got up to go to the bathroom, she whispered, 'Darling, as long as you've tasted it.' Then Douchebag D went to the bathroom too, and the Creep took the opportunity to ask me what I was good at. 'You mean in school?' I asked. 'I wouldn't dare to ask further,' he said and gave me that little smile again. I'm telling you, that Awfully Famous Author was one dirty bastard.

'Darling, as long as you've tasted it' was a sentence I thought about a lot later. I'd tasted being a muse, and I wanted to vomit it up like my calamari. At one point I mentioned this to Douchebag D: 'I'm so afraid of ending up like the Creep's wife.' He said *he'd never allow* that to happen, a statement that I found far from reassuring. These things did eventually play a role in my decision to break up with him. Moreover, I considered it a bad sign that, during dessert, I was already dreading the moment we'd take off our clothes. I think Douchebag D may have sensed this. He said, 'It's not so much that I want to shag you, I just want to *be* with you.'

We were actually pretty good at *being*. I don't think anybody has ever closed the doors and windows as thoroughly as Douchebag D did back then. Together, he and I inhabited a tiny world, filled with Bob Dylan, the song 'Paris 1919' by John Cale, and thoughts that never went beyond seeking recognition and the fear that it would never come.

Douchebag D really helped me overcome that fear. He even wrote me a letter about it: 'Stay calm, follow your intuition

23

and don't waste minutes or thoughts on the Others, Expectations or Ambitions. The Others don't exist, they'll fade away, their opinions are completely irrelevant. Forget them. Only be ashamed of things you should actually be ashamed of. For the rest: never walk in the shoes of your enemy.'

I didn't quite understand what he meant by that last sentence. Nor did I understand the sentence before it. But the rest – pretty useful advice. The only problem was that I didn't realize that the Others were, in fact, him. It was him I wanted to overcome, him and my brother, and maybe a few other people as well – in other words, the men. Don't get me wrong: men can be great human beings; I get along with plenty of them just fine. It's just that it so often goes *wrong*.

By *wrong* I mean that you often see these women with long, flowing hair and men with short hair, and somehow the women always end up with less room to breathe, with making jokes that people actually laugh at, with not having to smile all the time just so people don't think they're shrewish. That stuff can really get to me.

But I wasn't exactly aware of all this at the age of eighteen. Douchebag D and I liked to make jokes about all kinds of minorities, especially lesbians. For some reason, we thought they were really curious people. Once, after we'd broken up but he hadn't quite turned against me yet, we met up for coffee, and he told me that I'd become the bull dyke that we used to make fun of all the time. His words knocked the wind out of me. For those of you who have never been reduced to a cultural stereotype, that's what it feels like, like being punched in the gut so hard that you choke for a second. The annoying thing about it is that, due to the lack of air, you always end up offering the same response: a smile.

And so, when all was said and done, Douchebag D turned against me. It's a pretty tragic story, and I'm not sure we need to go into it. It started with the bull-dyke comment and ended with a whole bunch of other comments along those lines. Come to think of it, it ended where it always ends: with a 'just kidding' and 'come on, you can take it'.

I thought a lot about those jokes and why I was always the *you* at the butt of them. Maybe there was nothing wrong with the joke itself – maybe it was more the fact that the 'I's and the 'you's were so unevenly divided. I tried to explain this to him, but he didn't get it. That's the thing about people who've been 'I's for too long: they're never going to become 'you's. He called me a lesbian fundamentalist, and I guess maybe I am. But fundamentalists are always good for a laugh. Believe me.

Jennifer

The period after Douchebag D was a time marked by silence. I was living in a shipping container that didn't even *have* windows. There was just a front and a back door. The back door opened on to a balcony, which was loaded with beer crates left over from a house party I'd thrown. Hardly anybody came to my house party, so of course nothing much happened to the beers either.

Nobody ever came by because I wanted to be *alone*. I wanted to be one of the Greats. It was the same thing I'd wanted before, back when I was forgetting my orders at Bagels & Beans, but now I wanted it even more, even harder. Douchebag D had once said that if you read and write for two hours every day, within one or two years you'll get there. If Douchebag D did it for two hours, then I had to do it for three.

For days, weeks, months, I sat with my back against the

fridge reading books, books that I really didn't care about, because honestly I was more interested in my *own* contours, and that's not the way to find them. At least, for me it wasn't. The only book I got anything out of was *Youth* by J. M. Coetzee. It was about a boy who was doing exactly the same thing I was doing and feeling pretty depressed about it too.

My sexuality was non-existent at this point. I wasn't actually seeing anyone. Despite all my fears of turning into the Creep's wife, I couldn't shake the thought that Douchebag D was the best I'd ever have – and Douchebag D was out of the picture. I saw no one and kissed no one, because I thought that before long they'd want me to kiss them down there and then throw a towel at me afterwards. And that's what I *really* didn't want.

Come to think of it, I did kiss one guy, Koos – out on the balcony with all the beers. But before I knew it, he was sending me all kinds of Polish poems and whispering that he had always thought I was way out of his league. That's just not my thing. I'm not sure it's anyone's thing.

Koos studied Polish, and I knew him because I'd started studying Russian, which I wouldn't recommend to anyone. I'll tell you more about that later, but for now, just don't do it. Don't study Russian. It's like an army, but for people who'd rather not get off their chair.

Personally, I was having one anxiety attack after another. I just couldn't *do* it any more, you know? It wasn't just Russian – in hindsight, the whole programme didn't really play a significant role in my life – but more *in general*. I just couldn't do it any more. I was living – as I often described it in my secret writing sessions – entirely in my own echo. When you live in your own echo, all you can see and hear is yourself, and after a while you can't help but wonder if you're starting to lose it. What *it* is, you're not quite sure, and that only adds to the anxiety.

I was so anxious. Good God. I was anxious before class, anxious after class, anxious when I got up in the morning, anxious on my bike. *Anxiety is all the white which doesn't disappear into the line*, I wrote once. The only person I'd ever heard say anything meaningful on this topic was my philosophy teacher. He made the distinction between anxiety and fear: fear is about something concrete, whereas anxiety is the sensation that comes with the thought that *shit is going down*. My teacher joked that it was basically the feeling he got when he drank too much coffee. I had that feeling all the time.

Shit went down at the end of August, in the summer after my first year of Russian. I wrote a short piece about this once. I can share it with you if you want. It's called *Wibaut*.

Wibaut

I was cycling down Wibautstraat and saw the big dark clouds gathering overhead and realized that things were about to go wrong. Things went wrong a lot, to varying degrees. But this was: different.

I had eaten red beets from Hema that day. I cycled through Betondorp and wondered which street Johan Cruyff had lived on. I'd just been at a birthday party for someone

I didn't care for and noticed that Evelien wasn't smiling. My mother whispered, 'They just found out that Jona isn't going to get better.'

This was before we heard that *my* mother wasn't going to get better either – something I really wouldn't have been able to deal with at the time. That is, of course, the most tragic part: someone finds out that it's all going to end, and the only thing other people are sad about is the way it will go on for them.

The evening before I cycled down Wibautstraat, I'd gone to the movies by myself to see *Good Will Hunting*. I couldn't help but cry when Sean Maguire says to Will Hunting: 'It's not your fault, it's not your fault, it's not your fault.' That line still makes me cry, by the way.

The next day, I was on my way to a movie starring Viggo Mortensen. While I was sitting in the cinema, I heard all kinds of voices in my head – the voice of my brother, the voice of Douchebag D. As if they were giving some kind of speech. It was my funeral. I saw them standing behind one of those lecterns, a bit dazed but determined to give a good speech.

After the movie, I wanted to go home, but when I got to Waterlooplein I stopped. I needed to cry and called my brother. He didn't answer. He rarely picked up the phone, which is probably why I called him. I also considered calling Fenna, and my parents, but I didn't dare. My belief that I was drowning had been growing every day, but I hadn't told anyone. Then the moment you're about to go under, you don't dare to pick up the phone. So I just pedalled on.

I was living in an apartment complex made of shipping containers. Mine was on the second floor, and when I stood on the balcony, I could see up to the fifth. On the fifth floor there was a staircase to the roof. I looked at that staircase a lot. I knew that you could go up that staircase and never have to come back. Of course, I didn't want to do that, but then again, people who are afraid of heights don't want to jump either, they're afraid to *want* to jump.

When I got home I put *Everything Is Love* on and focused all my attention on it. Later I went to bed and thought briefly about the fact that the end actually has no end. But that thought always makes me nauseous, not from disgust but from the depth of it. Then I fell asleep, because back when I started having these kinds of thoughts at the age of ten, I'd promised myself only to think about them in sunny moments.

Sad story, right? After that night, I lived in the container for another week, but then – and this is the stupidest thing – I stopped being able to swallow. When you're extremely anxious, you eventually stop being able to swallow. You can't get anything down, but you keep rushing to the bathroom because that same feeling gives you diarrhoea. I lost six and a half pounds in one week, and that's when I realized it was time to go home.

I moved back in with my parents, where my mother just kept saying, 'Honey, it hurts me so much to *see* you like this.'

That really put me on edge. But at least there were no stairs, you know? That was the one thing I knew for sure: stay away from the stairs, because one day you'll want to come back. Sometimes, when you're blinded to all light, it's the only thing you can say to yourself: this will pass. You don't really believe it, but you know you *have* to.

A few months later, I was still deep in that darkness when I met my first girlfriend, Jennifer. Jennifer is an actress, though you've probably never heard of her. People have never heard of most actors: it's a misconception about them. The night I met her that was the first thing she said to me actually: 'You've probably never heard of me.' I found it an incredibly touching opening line and I don't think anyone has ever introduced themselves to me so candidly before.

The first thing I said to her was that I didn't know where the toilet was, and then I asked if she happened to be into girls. She pointed to the back. 'Yes,' she said. 'Then my name is Sofie,' I replied. When I came back from the toilet, she was still standing in the same spot. That's how I knew she wanted to kiss me. We started talking about her overalls, about which she said, 'These aren't lesbian dungarees. I'm just a lesbian in dungarees. Which is something else entirely.' It's weird, but lesbians are always very afraid of being lesbians. Probably because if they make one wrong move, they'll be labelled a fundamentalist.

But Jennifer didn't make any wrong moves. I asked her what she was drinking, and she said, 'Vodka and apple juice.' I tasted it, and it was exactly how the rest of the evening would taste: sweet and terribly strong. I stuck to beer myself and drank an awful lot of it. It was my first night at De Trut, and I didn't know much about De Trut, but I knew enough to know that a place whose name was literally 'The Bitch' wasn't going to leave anybody standing.

Come to think of it, nobody had any clothes on. The people working behind the bar were all practically naked, and pretty soon so were all the people on the dance floor. In that moment, I knew that this was exactly as it should be – and, somehow, it was as if I'd always known it. Fenna took it pretty hard. Fenna was my best friend, and she still is. Early on in the evening, she plopped down on a chair in the corner of the room, and every time I went over to check on her, she'd say, '*Dude*.' Then I'd hand her another beer and say, '*Bro*.' It's funny, but Fenna and I have always been able to say an awful lot with just these two words.

I don't know if I fell in love with Jennifer that night or not. Infatuation is a funny thing. But *damn* – I know I wanted to kiss her. It was as if she'd been drawn to mathematical perfection: her eyes with a compass, her jawline with a triangular ruler. 'I'm not going to kiss you,' she said, 'because then you'll think that all girls kiss like I do.' I told her I didn't care about that, that I wanted to kiss *her* and nobody else, and that was the truth.

We started making out, and I'm pretty sure it went on for several hours. I kissed her everywhere: on her neck, in her ear, on her nose. She whispered that she wanted to make fried eggs for me in the morning, and I remember wanting to fuck her, and that I'd never wanted that before, not *really*. Fenna had gone home by then. I didn't talk to her again until the next morning, on the phone. 'Hell of a night,' she said.

And it really was. When De Trut closed and literally *everyone* was naked except for me and Jennifer, Jennifer gave me her number. I wanted to give her my number, but she said, 'You call *me*.' On the way home I stopped my bike at the top of the steep little bridge that leads to Tweede Constantijn Huygensstraat and pulled down my pants to pee. Suddenly I thought that this must be the beginning. Only later did I understand that there is no beginning, for a moment it just *is* – happiness.

A week later we met at the Vesper cocktail bar. I was so nervous that after twenty minutes I went into the ladies' room and lay down on my back on the floor. I couldn't take it any more – it wasn't just Jennifer, who looked even better in jeans than she did in dungarees, it was also the price of the cocktails. I had called Daniel beforehand to ask him where to take a woman on a date. 'A cocktail bar,' he said firmly. This might actually explain the lack of women in my brother's life, because cocktail bars are ridiculously expensive. When I returned, Jennifer was being hit on by the bartender. Half an hour later we started kissing, and he tried to hit on both of us. Wherever Jennifer and I made out, we got hit on. Usually it'd get all quiet at first, then they'd smile – and then it'd start. Super weird when you think about it. Us being together always seemed to be taken as some kind of invitation. I had no interest in inviting *anyone*. But Jennifer said, 'Sof, that's just the way it goes.'

After Vesper, we went to Café Thijssen, where you could get

drunk without ending up in debt counselling. I think that's where Jennifer asked me for the first time what I did. I told her I wanted to write but didn't dare. She said, 'If you really want to write, you should just do it.' There was no arguing with that, and when she asked me if I wanted to go home with her, I said, 'I think so.' She ran her hands through my hair and said, 'Just for a cup of tea.'

When we got to her kitchen, she asked if a glass of water was okay instead, because otherwise her roommate would be woken up by the sound of the kettle boiling. Her roommate's name was Amélie, and she was the lover of a famous, but idle, ceramic artist. The potter's wife knew exactly what was going on, and she always referred to Amélie as 'the little witch'. But to me, Amélie was just Amélie.

I only saw the potter once – when I was walking into the bathroom and he was walking out. I ducked behind a cabinet but still managed to get a good look at him. Gorgeous upper body, that man had.

In bed, Jennifer and I started kissing again, and after about five minutes I tried to go down on her. I was dying to do it – to go down on someone. I remember being down there with my head between her legs, and all of a sudden I heard my mother's voice: 'Honey, it hurts me so much to *see* you like this.' Sometimes I really think of the wrong things at the wrong time. But before I could pull down her zipper, Jennifer grabbed me by the collar. 'You've never done this before, you little daredevil,' she said. Then we started kissing again. With women, it's easier to take things slow. Moreover, they'll rarely ask you to kiss anything specific and never throw a towel at you. If you're still not sure who you want to sleep with – well, you know where I stand.

Soon I was introduced to Jennifer's friends, and they were all actresses too. Every single one of them was drop-dead gorgeous, and I often wondered what I was doing hanging out with them. I'm pretty sure they were all wondering the same thing. They hardly said a word to me. Actors, I discovered, only talk to other actors. Everybody else is just a spectator – they don't see you, they only see your eyes. This is true for all actors and actresses, and it doesn't matter if you've heard of them or not.

Jennifer and her friends were *women* women, if you know what I mean. I wasn't. Occasionally, I'd cross my legs and sit like a lady too, if only for a second, but then Jennifer would say, 'You're overplaying it.' So at some point I just stopped. I stopped doing everything – stopped straightening my hair, stopped wearing lacy underwear, the lot. Suddenly, I had more oxygen, and that's what I remember most about Jennifer – she came as a blissful breath of fresh air.

Jennifer's best friend's name was Valentin, and he didn't speak to me either. Not because he was an actor, but because his little brother was extremely sick. I never really got to know Valentin. At least, that's what Jennifer said, 'That's not Valentin, that's his grief.' Valentin's grief consisted of a lot of GHB and a lot of men. Sometimes we'd go out together, and before I'd even hung up my coat Valentin was in somebody's arms. On nights like this, we'd occasionally exchange a few words.

He would offer me his glass and say, 'Sip for Sofie,' and as soon as it was on my lips, he'd add, 'Darling, there's a *fuckload* of GHB in there.' And I'd pass it back to him.

Valentin often stayed the night at Jennifer's place, because he didn't exactly have a home. There were a lot of guys who wanted him, though, and running them off via the intercom had become Jennifer's day job. They'd ring the doorbell at all hours of the day – sometimes crying, sometimes raging. Occasionally, all of a sudden, it would be the potter. Amélie would shuffle out of her room with an irritable expression because she'd just started watching a series. Amélie was doing her residency at the time, and I was terrified that one day she'd actually have to operate on me, because she clearly cared a lot more about *Gossip Girl* than about human lives.

It was a strange household: everyone *lay around*. Amélie in bed with her laptop, Valentin on the couch with a hangover and sometimes a ridiculously attractive boy, and me in Jennifer's bed because I was afraid of all these people and didn't dare to leave her room. Come to think of it, Jennifer was the only one who actually got up from time to time, usually to squeeze kiwis. Don't ask me why, but Jennifer more or less *lived* on kiwi juice.

After she'd brought everyone a glass of juice, she'd lie back down beside me in bed. Then she'd start kissing me and say, 'Just relax.' But I couldn't relax. In fact, all I could do was gaze at her endlessly and say, 'The woman behind the bar thinks you're the prettiest girl in De Trut.'

'I don't want the bartender to say it – I want *you* to say it,' she replied. And of course she was right. But I've always had a hard time getting into direct contact with people. Skydiving, no problem. Performing in front of a large audience, easy. But direct contact, no way. Eventually, I think Jennifer started to feel lonely because of all this. And I would have loved to have said, 'This isn't you, this is me,' but of course I didn't say that either.

You can imagine whatever you want about the lives of actresses, but they pretty much do just one thing: drink cappuccino. I swear – cappuccino, cappuccino, cappuccino. People usually associate actresses with movies, but it's not like that. Carice van Houten is in movies. The rest of them are stressing about auditions, which may or may not come.

Whenever Jennifer did manage to land an audition, it was usually for the role of a heterosexual teenager. According to Jennifer, once they put you in a box, you never got out of it. She was in the 'heterosexual-teenager' box. One of her friends was in the 'plus-size' box, and after she lost a ton of weight, they asked her to kindly put it on again – otherwise there weren't enough heavyweights to go around.

Eventually, Jennifer landed a good role in a play called *Polleke*, based on the children's book. She played this devious character who pretends to be Polleke's best friend, but who later, at a crucial moment in the story, kisses Mimoen, Polleke's crush. It kind of made me mad, really, because Polleke was dealing with a lot of shit at that point. If you asked me, they'd have been better off casting Amélie, you know?

I googled the book that the play was based on and found

a book report written by a high-schooler. It read: 'I didn't like this book at all. It was sad and boring, because nothing really happens. It was also sad because most of the story was centred around the death of Polleke's grandfather. It was also pretty childish too. Even though Polleke was already twelve, she still did a lot of stupid things and was really bad at writing poems even though she thought she was good at it. The book was educational because it was about faith and the fact that everyone believes in something. But faith isn't really a topic that interests me.'

Total bullshit, if you ask me. I thought Polleke's poems were great: 'The eyes of the cow / Are sad and wise / Tired, almost glum / As if she's made a long trip / And knows: here I shouldn't have come.' This is a beautiful poem, and anyone who doesn't believe so clearly doesn't believe in anything.

People always say you should steer clear of actresses before opening night, and it's true. Jennifer hardly spoke to me. She stopped wanting sex – at least not *real* sex. Real sex involves a lot of kissing, at least in my opinion. But she didn't want kisses, she just wanted me to finger the hell out of her. Nothing makes me sadder than having to do that. I did it, of course; I did it really long and really hard, and I hoped that it might wake her up. But it didn't wake her up, not *really*.

I met her parents at the premiere, and the only thing her mother said to me was, 'I imagined you with long hair.' Her mother was the worst: the kind of person who says it's wonderful when her daughter turns out to be into women but wants to throw herself off a cliff when she finds out the girl she's dating is so noticeably a lesbian. I am noticeably a lesbian, and there's nothing I can do about it. My look changed around that time and I'm telling you, there's not an opinion out there that I haven't heard.

One of the most frequent comments is: 'You know, you don't have to cut off all your hair just because you're a lesbian.' It's a strange kind of logic. What they really mean is, 'For Christ's sake, don't cut off all your hair, otherwise everyone will know you're a lesbian and then maybe your girlfriend's mum won't speak to you any more.' This logic is strange too, but at least it's more honest.

After the show, I didn't feel like standing next to Jennifer's parents in silence, so I decided to wander around the building. I felt kind of like that sad cow that Polleke was talking about, you know? I just kept thinking: Here I shouldn't have come.

In the end, we all went out for dinner together: Jennifer, her parents, the actress Sallie Harmsen and me. Sallie Harmsen was the lead, and she definitely knew it. I know it's not very nice to say, but of all the actresses I'd met, Sallie Harmsen was the absolute worst. I think I introduced myself to her thirty-four times, and every single time she nodded with incredible interest when I said my name. The next time I see her, I think I'll just tell her my name is Sallie Harmsen. Maybe then she'll remember it.

The day after the premiere, Jennifer broke up with me. It was all very clinical, and later there were times when I wished I could break up with people the same way, but I never could. Sometimes it occurs to me that Sallie Harmsen might have whispered the idea in her ear, though that's pretty unlikely. I don't think Sallie Harmsen even knew I had a thing with Jennifer; she probably thought I was her accountant. People are generally nicer about breaking up with their accountants than Jennifer was with me, by the way.

You know what she said? She said she just wanted to put all the annoying things in her life behind her. And now that opening night was over, it was my turn. I wanted to scream at her that she was a heterosexual teenager, 'And you always will be!' But I don't do that to people. I just begin to have difficulty swallowing and wait for the diarrhoea to begin.

What is this, *Blue Is the Warmest Colour*?

Blue Is the Warmest Colour is a 2013 French film about a fifteen-year-old girl from Lille who falls madly in love with another girl. The first time I saw it, I had just broken up with Douchebag D, and I sobbed like a baby because it so perfectly captured the intense feeling of loneliness that comes after a break-up. In fact the film captures every feeling – or at least every feeling worth feeling – perfectly. If life were only three hours long, I would just turn on *Blue* – it covers everything there is to cover.

The movie's three hours and seven minutes long, so I guess in that case you would miss the last seven minutes. So I'll just tell you what happens: after an emotional break-up, Adèle goes to her ex's art exhibition and discovers that most of the paintings are of her. She meets the former love of her life's new girlfriend, who looks at her with big eyes and says, 'See? You're still here.'

Then this guy who appeared an hour earlier walks up. Obviously, he's been into Adèle from the beginning. He chats with her a bit until a friend taps him on the shoulder. At that, Adèle walks outside. In the next shot, we see the guy looking for her, but she's already left. She walks round the corner and lights a cigarette. Then the credits roll.

Okay, so maybe this doesn't sound like much, but if you'd seen the three hours leading up to this moment, you'd be bawling like I was. The most beautiful line in the entire film is, '*Je ne t'aime plus, mais j'ai une infinie tendresse pour toi, et je l'aurai toujours – pour toute ma vie,*' which translates as, 'I don't love you any more, but I have infinite tenderness for you, and I always will – for the rest of my life.' A truly beautiful sentence if you ask me. After I left the cinema, I wrote a letter to Douchebag D: 'I probably still love you, but above all I feel an infinite tenderness.'

Douchebag D wrote back that he was impressed with my writing, but he didn't say anything about the tenderness part. Maybe that was the moment when I decided to focus my energy on becoming a damn good writer and drop the whole tenderness thing.

I think I watched *Blue Is the Warmest Colour* about thirty-one times. There are some fairly explicit sex scenes in it, and the first time I saw them, I missed a lot. I always sit in the second row at the cinema because nobody ever sits there, and I can make all the weird faces I want. But on that particular afternoon there was a man sitting next to me, and whenever a sex scene started, he stared down at his toes. I'm a pretty environment-sensitive person, so when he looked down, I looked down too. As I'm already familiar with my own toes, I ended up staring at his.

When it was all over, I left the cinema knowing nothing more about lesbian sex, but a lot about a couple of toes that really didn't do it for me. But here's the thing: it doesn't matter if you stared at some guy's toes during all the sex scenes or kept your eyes glued to the screen, you would still wonder how much this movie actually tells us about lesbian sex. I, for one, don't know *anyone* who does it like Adèle and Emma did.

For starters, they're constantly going down on each other. Not me – I only go down on people *sometimes*. And there's this strange symmetry to their sex – as if they have to satisfy each other exactly the same way just because they belong to the same biological category. A load of crap if you ask me.

And when you *do* have less symmetrical sex, it's not because one person is 'the guy' and the other is 'the woman'. It's because one's named Marissa and the other's name is Lisan. That's why. I should add that I'm definitely the guy in bed, and the other person is definitely the woman – but that's not the case for *everybody*. Fucking heteros, you've got to teach them everything.

But there was a time when I didn't really get it either – sex I mean. After Jennifer kicked me out, I just wandered the streets for a while. I thought about that idle potter and Amélie and wondered which series she was watching. But mostly I thought about the sex I had had with Jennifer, and why I could never relax when she said, 'Just relax.'

I drew all kinds of conclusions, but the one that really stuck with me was that I wasn't good enough in bed, and that's what I needed to become – good. Or more precisely: *excellent*. I wanted to be a master. And if you want to master something, you need a good teacher. Suddenly, I realized that my teacher had been there all along – Rose.

Rose was the captain of my football team and a born leader. She always said, 'Lakmaker, get out of that *head* of yours!' That woman understood my head. Those are the best people – the ones who understand what's going on in your head and still know when to drag you out of it. Whenever I wasn't playing well in a match or whenever I left practice with my head low, she'd look me straight in the eye and say, 'Dushi, talk *real* with me.' Those are my kind of people, the ones you can be *real* with.

Rose had a gold tooth and a huge arse. She knew how to put that arse to work during training. And when you're up against an opponent with an arse as big as Rose's, I guarantee you that you'll never touch the ball again. After a while I started to notice that she kept tugging at my shirt. Not just when we were fighting for the ball, but when the ball was way over on the other side of the pitch. Well, *that* was one hell of a turn-on.

I'm not about to challenge any of the stereotypes about women's football here. Well, except the most obvious one – that women can't play. Women are absolutely brilliant at football. But otherwise, they're all lesbians, even when they say they're only *temporary* lesbians, they all spit, some even *snot rocket*. Pretty disgusting, huh? Almost as disgusting as stereotypes.

Lots of girls on our team were temporary lesbians. They'd find themselves a girlfriend, and say, 'I'm only into *her* – and men.' That kind of stuff makes me incredibly sad. People would rather die than be *only* into women. There were two girls on our team who were so scared of becoming lesbians that they avoided everyone and only hung out with each other. And yep, you guessed it – before long they were a hot item.

Still, for some reason, one of them kept blaming us. 'What is this, Henny Huisman's *Surprise Show*? Fucking *Stars in their Eyes*?' she'd say. I never really understood what a cheesy Saturday evening TV show had to do with it, but what she meant was: you went in as one person and came out as somebody completely different. And there was some truth to that.

The grey paving stones of the SC Buitenveldert sports complex were hallowed ground for lesbians. Rose and I even had sex in one of the toilet stalls. Actually, we wanted to do it in locker room 17, which was reserved for the top team, and they were sponsored by ING Bank. Everything was bright orange and it was the only locker room at Buitenveldert that didn't smell like foot fungus. But we couldn't use it because there was already a couple in there. Somebody should really tell ING that not only are they supporting arms trafficking in conflict zones, they're also bankrolling some serious girl-on-girl action.

The only person who knew about all this was Fred, our physio. He treated all the players on the first- and second-tier teams, and he massaged us so incredibly slowly that eventually every single one of us spilled our guts to him. He never asked questions; he just nodded. Fred was like the team's de facto counsellor. We had an official counsellor too – Gerrie – but people avoided him like the plague. He was always trying to get us to *dig deep*.

I think I was the one player at Buitenveldert who didn't mind digging deep. The only problem was that Gerrie and I wouldn't really be able to get back up again. In those moments, we'd gaze at each other intently and he'd say, 'Sof, you really need to stop thinking so much.' Here's a tip for counsellors – try to actually *engage* with people's thoughts before you tell them to shut up. If you like telling people to shut up, become a coach.

Gerrie was eventually fired after everyone agreed that he wasn't really helping. In his farewell speech, he talked about the match that we were set to play against Ajax the following week. 'Girls,' he said, 'this is a once-in-a-lifetime experience.' God, I'm so tired of people saying stuff like that. Don't tell me this is a once-in-a-lifetime experience. We played friendlies against professional teams all the time. There was nothing once-in-a-lifetime about it. But Gerrie always had to add an extra layer of gravity to things. Which was why everyone wanted him gone. He was like Wagner on pop radio. It just didn't *fit*.

I was sitting next to Rose during his speech, and while all eyes were on Gerrie, she started slowly squeezing my upper thigh. Not hard, but with feeling. Well, that got me all hot again, so after Gerrie was done I said, 'There's this Hungarian film I've been really wanting to see.' What I was really thinking was, 'Wanna fuck?' But believe it or not, I actually wouldn't say something like that out loud. Honestly – I just wouldn't dare.

A week later, we met at the Eye Film Museum. We were already late for the movie, and when we got to the entrance, the lady checking tickets stopped us because she didn't believe I was old enough. 'Son, this film is rated sixteen and up.' It was so weird. Not because she didn't believe I was sixteen – that happens all the time – but because she called me 'son'. I didn't even know people still say that. They just say 'sir' or 'dude' or something.

I showed her my cinema pass with my date of birth on it, but she wasn't convinced. So I pulled out my passport. Only then did she nod with a huge frown on her face. People always frown and nod when they look at my passport. I guess that's because they assumed I was a fifteen-year-old boy and are surprised to find out that I'm actually a woman in her mid-twenties. Sometimes they even think it's fake. 'That's a nice passport you got there, sonny,' they say. I've actually been thinking about having a fake passport made: 'Josiah Lakmaker, born in Amsterdam on 26 April 2005.' I wouldn't be able to buy beer with it, but at least I'd be normal. Some days that seems more valuable than beer.

In hindsight, I probably was too young for that movie, Rose too. *Son of Saul* is about a man forced to work in the Sonderkommando at Auschwitz in 1944. A little tip for first dates: don't go to a Sonderkommando movie. Don't do anything remotely related to Sonderkommandos. If I were you, I would just avoid Sonderkommandos altogether on a first date.

The papers called *Son of Saul* a reconstruction of hell, and that's pretty much what it was. Afterwards, when Rose asked me what I wanted to drink, I said, 'Nothing.' I had the same feeling I had after I read *If This Is a Man* by Primo Levi. I couldn't eat or drink after that book either. 'Death begins with the shoes,' he wrote. Prisoners who were given the wrong shoe size often died from problems that began in their feet. I spent the entire winter walking around the house barefoot just to feel a little bit of the cold they must have felt.

Strange, I know, and I didn't stop until my mother picked up on it. 'Have you *completely* lost your mind?' she asked. She named me after her grandmother who died in the gas chambers at Auschwitz on her birthday. That seems like a sure-fire way to ensure your child *completely* loses their mind if you ask me.

Rose lived on Mercatorplein, and when we got inside it looked like she had no furniture. 'I really like what you've done here,' I said when we walked in. But she'd already started kissing me. I thought we'd spend some time breaking the ice first, but for Rose there was no such thing as ice. 'Fuck me before my housemate gets home,' she said, which totally stressed me out. And you know what's funny? That roommate never *did* come home. Like never. Later, I started noticing a pattern – housemates who were never home. Where *are* all these people, for Christ's sake?

The only thing in the living room was a couch. She pushed me on to it and tore off her clothes. Sometimes when people talk about sex they say things like, 'It just happened' – basically my experience in a nutshell. Only for me it's more like watching *Son of Saul*, you know? All of a sudden, you're thinking, wait, what the hell is going on here? At least with *Son of Saul* you can just sit back and watch it happen. But with sex, you can't get away with that. They always want you to *participate* in sex. I really hate participating in sex.

While I sat on the couch, she shoved her breasts into my face. That part was nice. Rose has these incredibly massive breasts. I would've been happy just to stay there for ever. In my head, I was already thinking, okay, see you later. But sex doesn't work like that. She pulled her breasts back out of my face and asked, 'What do *you* like?'

Of all the questions in the world, that's probably the one I hate the most. If I'd been honest, I would've said, 'When you keep your goddamn hands to yourself.' But you just can't say that. That'd be like stopping in the middle of a match and saying, 'Excuse me, could you maybe just get that ball out of here?' You just *can't*. Try it.

Look, I can say all of this stuff to you now, but I couldn't say it to her back then. No way. So I tried to turn the question around by going down on her. Honestly, I don't really care what happens during sex – as long as *I'm* not there. I just needed somewhere to disappear to. And I know it might sound like I'm bragging here, but I actually made her come. And a few hours later, I did it *again*. That kind of thing makes me grin.

After she came for the second time, I started kissing her very

49

slowly. To me, kissing is a perfectly logical thing to do after sex. But Rose gave me a puzzled look. 'What are you doing?' she asked. 'I'm kissing you,' I said. Then she turned away. She sat upright and glared at me. 'What is this, *Blue Is the Warmest Colour*?' My god, lesbians – they know *exactly* which films to use to make a point.

To be honest, I wanted to cry, but I swallowed back the tears. Sometimes you can sort of swallow back your tears. You just focus all your thoughts on something else – the orange walls in locker room 17, for example – and push them back. But how to hold back tears wasn't what I was trying to learn from Rose, you know? Sometimes you can really pick up the wrong things from people.

Fuck Me, Lakkie

For those of you wondering what Rose and I look like in real life, we were in an episode of *The Pigeonhole Man* called 'The Lesbians', and yes, it was about lesbians. Rose is wearing very large sunglasses, and I'm wearing a hat. It caused quite a stir in the lesbian community when it aired. Everyone wanted to know – and these are their words, not mine – who was that chick in the hat? I think it was because I spoke in complete sentences. People aren't used to that, not on television.

After we shot the episode, the director came up to me and said, 'Finally, someone who speaks in complete sentences.' Complete sentences are my speciality, and when I speak in them, I prefer to do it in a hat.

Since everyone wanted to know who I was, they all asked Saskia Ketting. Saskia Ketting is the epicentre of the lesbian community. They* are like Utrecht Central Station for the

* Saskia Ketting is non-binary, and anyone who thinks this is ridiculous is ridiculous.

Amsterdam lesbian community. I know Saskia Ketting quite well – they belong to my inner circle. But that's not saying much: Saskia Ketting *is* the inner circle.

There was one woman in particular who asked Saskia Ketting about me early on. She needed to know where I was immediately. Believe it or not, Saskia Ketting was leading me into a trap. It was a blissful trap, but a trap nonetheless. They asked me if I could teach them the AKKA 3000. This is a very complicated football trick that probably none of you can do. I can, and if someone asks me to teach them, I take their request very seriously.

We met up in Westerpark, where I began calmly explaining to Saskia Ketting how the trick works. The AKKA 3000 consists of roughly seven steps, so there's a lot of theory involved. But just as I was kicking the ball up with a look of concentration on my face, Saskia Ketting started to grin. I turned round, and that's when I saw her: a woman cycling in pink heels and trousers with one transparent leg. Can you imagine? One of her trouser legs was see-through. 'I'm coming for you,' she said, and pedalled across the grass towards us.

It took me a second to figure out that nobody was here to learn the AKKA 3000. Even though it's such a cool trick. Pretty soon, Saskia said that they had to be somewhere and left me with the woman in pink heels. Her name was Kyra. I was wearing the hat again and said, 'You must be interested in my complete sentences.' 'Not really,' she replied.

Then I tried to pummel her with jokes, because that felt like my best bet at that point, but she wasn't impressed. She said: 'If I had to describe you, your sense of humour wouldn't be the first thing I'd mention.' It's those kinds of comments that give me a lump in my throat. So I got defensive and said, 'Why is your left trouser leg see-through?'

'That's none of your business,' she replied. And added that one of her trouser legs probably cost more than my monthly rent. She explained that she'd been on vacation in Brazil, and on the last day she had to choose between an afternoon of jet-skiing or these trousers. In the end, she thought, *Fuck it, whatever* and chose both. It was something that Kyra thought a lot – *Fuck it, whatever.* About almost everything, really. I guess that's what I liked about her so much. That and the left trouser leg, of course.

Things got a little messy between me and Kyra. The first five times I slept with her it was always in a different house. Apparently, her accountant was always telling her, 'Kyra, now's the time to buy,' but she didn't have a fixed address of any kind, so every now and then I'd mutter, 'Kyra, just *rent* a place.' Maybe she thought renting was too bourgeois. Kyra was terrified of being bourgeois, which I found a little bourgeois of her, to be honest. But what can I say, I grew up in Amsterdam Zuid in a part-Jewish family. After the Holocaust, they had more important things to worry about than whether renting was bourgeois. Especially when they already owned a house round the corner from the Concertgebouw.

On the fifth night, I told her I was dating a girl who was on the cover of Greek *Vogue*. Not quite the same as American *Vogue* or Dutch *Vogue*, but I was still pretty impressed. But sometimes it's better to just keep these things to yourself, no matter how impressed you are. Kyra told me to grab my stuff and get out. 'I'm not going to be your side bitch,' she said, and she had a point.

A week later I ran into her at a party at NYX. I spent half the night talking to a girl who thought she recognized me from TV. Naturally, I assumed she meant from *The Pigeonhole Man* and that she was going to ask me about my hat. But she didn't ask me that at all; she just hugged me and whispered that she was so moved by the scene with my parents. 'What did my parents say?' I asked. 'That they accept you the way you are,' she said with a smile.

After a while, it turned out that she was talking about a show about transgender people she'd seen called *He's a She*. It wasn't entirely clear to me if she thought I'd recently become a he or a she. It would actually have been nice if she'd told me. But we never got to it because I spotted Kyra standing in the middle of the room. When I said hello, she said, 'Hey Lak.' Kyra never called me Sofie – just Lak, Lakkie or Lakmaker, depending on the mood of our relationship, and that mood changed every fifteen minutes.

'Lak' was not a good sign. Then she asked, 'So how's Vogue?' I couldn't wait to tell her that Vogue had no sense of humour. Which was true – she didn't. We only went on one date, and all she talked about was how bad the Armenian genocide was. I mean, I agreed with her, of course, but it seemed like a pretty complicated topic for a first date. In fact, she was constantly

54

saying things that I could only nod to, such as, 'All my friends are very sweet people,' or 'I like to listen to Radiohead.'

I replied that I didn't have that many friends, so I liked to listen to Lil' Kleine because he sang stuff like: 'Fuck everyone if you can trust yourself.' Of course, I knew that this wasn't great for my image, but I was hoping it would rile her a bit. But there was no riling her, not Vogue.

Kyra, on the other hand, was easy to rile. Honestly, she was riled all the time. At NYX, she told me that I had left my Ajax lunchbox at her place. It's pathetic, I know, but I still use lunchboxes. She said I could come by and pick it up that night, and after that she didn't want to see my face ever again. That's the funny thing about Kyra, when she says she never wants to see your face again what she really means is that you're welcome to come over. It's when she says you're welcome that you should worry.

Over breakfast, I told her that she should come over to my place sometime so she could see just how incredibly tasteful it was. I shouldn't have said that. Like really – I absolutely should not have said that. The first time she visited, she hauled two-thirds of my furniture out on to the street. Before I forget, I should mention that Kyra worked as an art director in the film industry. I can't deny it – she had really good taste. But after that afternoon, my house was basically empty, and later that week she broke up with me, so we couldn't look for new furniture either.

I'm not going to lie, it was a really rough time. All I had left was a bed and a kitchen sink. If they would've fitted through the stairwell, Kyra would've thrown them out too. It had a very disruptive effect. People get pretty attached to their stuff. Maybe that's the most important lesson I learned from Kyra: never get attached – there's nothing that can't be hauled out to the pavement.

One rainy afternoon, I heard a beep outside my door. It was Kyra, and she had two announcements: one, we were back on, and two, she'd picked up a ton of new stuff for me at a warehouse. My house has been stylish ever since. Sometimes I still like to warn people, 'Watch out, this place was decorated by Kyra the art director' – that way, no one would ever dream of hauling my stuff out on to the street again.

Kyra had a fairly high but variable income. The film industry – *oh boy*. Talk about strange people. Everyone speaks of art in a serious tone, and you can tell by the look in their eyes that they're all terrified of losing their jobs due to budget cuts. But that literally never happens. They all earn shitloads of money. If you ask me, people in the film industry are all convinced that the only way to become a real artist is to be screwed over by the state.

Getting screwed over by the state does have an artistic edge to it, I'll give them that. But people in the film industry mostly get screwed over by each other. They're constantly making phone calls, trying to persuade each other to collaborate on things. You know what film people spend most of their days doing? Drinking lattes and delighting in the possibility of new collaborations. The rest of the time, they're making commercials for ING Bank.

Kyra did a commercial for ING once. They filmed it just round the corner from my place. In the middle of the afternoon, she knocked on my door because her leek was falling apart. She had made a two-metre-long leek to be tied to the roof of a car. We stuck my mop in it for stability, and I followed her back to the set out of curiosity. Do you know what the leek was for? Nothing. 'Oh, that looks fantastic!' the director exclaimed. That's one thing I really can't stand – useless props. The entire commercial consisted of a car driving away after a ridiculously attractive man gives it a little tap on the hood. That's it. These are the kinds of storylines that people in the advertising industry have to work with. The rest of the time they're sitting around drinking lattes.

But I can't really complain. I've certainly benefited from Kyra's income. We went out for dinner so often that I know all of the menus in downtown Amsterdam by heart. Every time we had a fight and threatened to break up, Kyra would say, 'Oh fuck it Lak, let's go out for dinner.' And I would nod.

Our fights usually started like this: we'd be walking down the street, me not saying anything (because I knew that if Kyra had to describe me, my sense of humour wouldn't be the first thing she'd mention) and Kyra nodding with growing rage. 'Lakmaker, I'm calling a taxi,' she'd say suddenly. A lot of people would take that as a sign that the conversation was over, but with us it meant that I needed to listen up. I don't think I listened very well. I just loved being with her because she knew something I rarely did: where to go.

Kyra *always* knew where to go, whether she was in her white

57

van, which had long since been banned in the city centre due to its emissions, or wearing heels so high that any other human being would break their ankles in them. My destination wasn't hers, I understood that, but I cherished every minute I spent in that passenger seat. When it was all over, I'd be adrift again, that much I knew.

Once we went out to a super-expensive restaurant where you didn't get to choose what you ate. Apparently, that's the epitome of luxury – a lack of choice. You just indicated whether you wanted six or seven courses, and I think we went for seven. I think the idea behind eating so many courses is that the dishes are all very light, so you can actually eat every-thing. Now I have all kinds of positive things to say about the food and the ambience of the place, but nothing there was light – *nothing*.

Our third dish was a pigeon stuffed to the brim with pesto, and the main course was still to come. I suggested to Kyra that we donate it to charity, but she wouldn't hear of it. By the time we reached the first dessert, I started to feel dizzy, and that's when we were approached by a man who had been sitting a few tables away from us.

He said, 'You two make a strikingly beautiful pair.' My god – men. Why can't they just stay at their own table? Either they'll ask to *join* you, or they'll give you an earful. But if you're in a really fancy restaurant, they hit you with lines like that. If central government really wanted to do something to support us, they should make those NO LEAFLETS, NO JUNK

MAIL stickers for lesbians. Although two 'No's generally isn't enough.

The reason we were out for dinner in the first place was that Kyra was headed off to shoot a feature film in Slovakia. As a kid, there was this book I absolutely loved by Jacques Vriens about a little boy who lived in a hotel where everyone was always fighting. Well, it could've just as easily been about Kyra and her colleagues on the film set. In that fancy hotel in Bratislava, everybody fought with everybody. Especially about the budget. The budget was the responsibility of some woman named Hanneke, but she never made it to Bratislava – she was stuck at home in Amsterdam with tinnitus. The cameraman, the sound technicians, the actors – they all wanted more money. And since Hanneke wasn't there to strangle, they grabbed each other's throats. Film people, I'm telling you – *absolutely nuts*, every last one of them.

After a month, Kyra had me flown in, because it turned out that her budget wasn't so tight after all. You're probably hoping that I'm going to tell you something about movies and how they're really made. Unfortunately, I have to disappoint you. Pardon my French, but Kyra and I did nothing but fuck in Slovakia.

Fucking, fucking and more fucking: that was it. We barely even ate. The first time we slept together in Slovakia, Kyra started to cry. 'I'm not feeling it,' she said. Kyra's crying fits had become a regular fixture in our sex life. Sometimes she cried because she wasn't feeling it, sometimes she cried because she was feeling *everything*. Once she cried because I was taking too long to find her clitoris. 'Lakkie,' she said, 'there's something not right between you and my clitoris.'

The clitoris and I do have a bit of a complex relationship. It's a complexity that I, depending on how you look at it, never quite conquered. Kyra wasn't allowed to touch me any more, at least not *there*. And not my breasts either, though sometimes she'd insist: 'But Lak, there's definitely *feeling* there.' Feeling, my arse. You know what it is? People get so worked up about stuff, especially in bed, when it's not even about them. It was never about them, it has always been about me, and if you really want the truth – I've had moments where I'd rather jump in the Amstel. The Amstel wouldn't even notice me. The river wouldn't have any girlfriends to whisper about me with or future lovers who'll be more easy-going than me. All this time, all I've wanted is the Amstel, but I've never been able to say it out loud.

Until I met Kyra, I think, because she's the one who started it, all the talking. I think it was at the seventh house on the seventh bed when she asked, 'Lak, love, is there something *wrong*?' And the worst thing about it is that, even then, I didn't even say *yes*, I never actually said *yes*. I just didn't say *no*, time and time again – I didn't say *no*. When it comes down to it, being silent is my speciality, and when I do it, I prefer to do it naked.

II

THE HISTORY OF
MY BEING WRONG

Everybody's Depressed

I realize that there's a huge part of my history that I haven't told you about. That's the problem with sex: once you start talking about it, it's really hard to stop. It gets more attention than it deserves, I think. The truth is, sexuality is like plumbing: super-annoying when it's out of order, and you can't really live without it. But obviously life's not all about plumbing. You get what I'm saying?

If you don't, it's fine. We didn't all study philosophy. I did study philosophy, which is why I'm good at abstract thinking and see connections between things like plumbing and sexuality. These connections aren't really there, but I still see them. It's the kind of thing you learn when you study philosophy, which is why most people who graduate in philosophy can't find a job. The world prefers to work with existing connections, the ones that people actually agree on.

People who spend their days pondering connections that

the rest of the world doesn't see are generally very lonely – and sometimes a little crazy. That's how most of the people in the philosophy department were: very lonely, and sometimes a little crazy. Actually, everyone was depressed, and that's what really got to me. Hunched, that's how they walked. Hunched with their pale faces to the ground, pondering connections that they didn't fully understand but still found plausible. In philosophy, nothing was ever as it was. Everything was always 'plausible'.

One of the first classes that I took in philosophy was logic. The teacher kept telling me that I should sign up for the honours programme. The honours programme is for students with an inferiority complex, who think that they'll only ever be honoured if they participate in something with the word 'honour' in it. Which is why I told the teacher that the honours programme was for losers. 'Strictly speaking, one cannot determine whether the honours programme is for losers until one is on the honours programme,' he replied. These are the kinds of conversations you have *all the time* with people who teach or study logic.

The required reading for the course was *Tractatus Logico-Philosophicus* by Wittgenstein. Nobody understood a word of it, which I actually found pretty funny. Wittgenstein says in the preface that his book is only for people who've already had similar thoughts. Then, at the end, he says that anyone who has truly understood the contents of the book should realize that it is in fact senseless and superfluous.

That said, I still thought it was a beautiful book. In my

opinion, you don't always have to understand something to find it beautiful. I think Wittgenstein really wanted to be right, and only after he had all the rightness on his side did he see that being right wasn't such a big deal. I guess it's kind of like the honours programme: when you're finally right, you see that being right is for losers.

Being right really *is* for losers, and I think they should've made that a bit clearer during the departmental open house. Especially to all the white *boys*. My god — white boys. Constantly saying, 'Well, yes, *but . . .*', 'Well, yes, but ma'am . . .', 'Well, yes, but sir . . .' I swear, it was non-stop.

A philosophy class looked like this: anxious girls frantically taking notes and marking passages with their highlighter — don't ask me why, but girls always have highlighters — and boys staring off into space and, when it suited them, raising their hand to say, 'Well, yes, but . . .' They usually didn't get much further than that.

And then there was me, of course. I was terrible too. Insufferable — that's what I was. You want to know what I thought? I always thought that people had trouble *expressing themselves*. Professors, students — everybody. So, whenever somebody said something, I'd say exactly the same thing, but better. Believe me, it was enough to drive any bystander absolutely nuts.

After the first year you were allowed to choose your own courses, so I chose one on critical social theory. I'm pretty critical by nature, and society suits me fine. But I soon discovered that the entire class was devoted to feminism, and the most uncomplicated kind of feminism at that. Uncomplicated feminism could be summed up as follows: 'White heterosexual highly educated women are also allowed to speak.' Chances are they probably wanted to call the course that at first, but there was some committee that needed time to decide whether or not it was accurate.

In philosophy, world history was in fact divided into thirty-six PowerPoint slides, one of which contained people of colour and women. It was usually a very nice slide, and I wouldn't have wanted to be represented anywhere else. It was also the *rowdiest* slide, which is probably why they always clicked through it rather quickly.

Critical social theory was an odd class. For starters, there was almost no one in it. There were only six of us, and the only one who ever said anything was this girl who cursed like a sailor. 'In-fucking-justice, man!' Stuff like that. Sometimes she came to class with a hangover. On those days, she was less talkative. But she'd still point out things that she thought were 'un-fucking-fair'. Both were good names for the course, if you ask me.

Our teacher always looked shocked whenever the girl opened her mouth, and was probably trying to figure out what Simone de Beauvoir would have done in her position. Our teacher had been re-reading *The Second Sex* for about forty years and had become, for that reason, a little aloof. *The Second Sex* is this thick book that basically says that women are allowed to speak too. Personally, I don't need nine hundred pages to be told that, but naturally a book like that has to be examined *in light of its time*. Really, everything in philosophy has to be examined *in light of its time*, which got pretty exhausting after a while. It would have been nice if we could've examined things in light of *my* time for once.

Nevertheless, there were certain philosophers who left a deep impression on me. You know who left a deep impression on me? Theodor Adorno. Theodor Adorno said that we were all a bunch of lazy fascists who should read a book instead of going to the movies all the time. If you ask me, the man had a point. Basically, it comes down to this: Wittgenstein said language was right, Simone de Beauvoir said women were right, and Adorno said suffering was right. The truth is hidden in suffering, and whoever opens their eyes to suffering will find it – rightness.

The man who taught us this was tall and bald, exactly the kind of person I can't help but take seriously. He would pace back and forth across the classroom, and with such long legs, he was always just a step or two away from the opposite wall. I think it started to get to him after a while, because his face would become more serious as the class went on. How exactly he looked nobody knew because he never made eye contact. I like people like that – unfit for society. Only once did he say something that wasn't about Adorno, and that was when he was about to become a father. 'I'm expecting offspring,' he grumbled, and then sank even deeper into thought. My kind of person.

I'm always telling people, 'Oh, I've got loads of friends from my philosophy days.' In fact I have no friends *at all* from those days. The only people I met there were weasels; every one of them born on the Leidsekade. Of all the weasels I met in the philosophy department, there are two I'll tell you about: the Mütsel brothers. Their names were Herman and Lodewijk Mütsel – actually, those weren't their real names, but they're very well connected in the legal world. I'm not one to shy away from risk, but I'm not going to risk *everything*.

Lodewijk Mütsel hadn't brushed his teeth in years, and Herman was a groper. It might seem like these things have nothing to do with each other, but they do: everyone born on the Leidsekade is so convinced of their own purity that they actually think they can spend their whole lives rolling around in the dirt without ever having to be confronted by it. Unfortunately, there's some truth to this – the world decides very early in life who's clean and who's dirty.

At every house party I went to, Lodewijk Mütsel was there too, walking around with this dirty smile on his face. His yellow teeth were remarkably far apart, and he had this incredibly greasy head of hair. Kind of like a troll, actually, a troll sniffing around. If I was talking to a girl, and she and I managed to slip out of his field of vision, he would come and find me afterwards. Then he'd grab the fingers on my right hand and sniff them.

Pussy or tangerine: that was the name of the game. I never showed any interest whatsoever in participating, but boys born on the Leidsekade are generally not concerned with matters of consent. So that's what he did: he *sniffed* my middle and index fingers and decided what they smelled like. Pretty disgusting, huh?

But Herman Mütsel was even more disgusting. He groped girls left and right, but at parties like these he'd go around talking about *contemporary feminism*. Nobody understood a word of it. It was all very confusing, and to add to the confusion he'd give these speeches peppered with words like *de jure* and *de facto*. Nobody got that either. Herman, you're a monster both *de jure* and *de facto*, I'd think to myself. But, of course, I never said it out loud. Actually, I never confronted him about his behaviour at all. Truth is, I'm a coward. I'm not cut from good wood, I'm cut from veneer from IKEA: the crappiest kind – it can hardly be called wood at all.

I should mention that Herman Mütsel and I were both in love with the same girl. He, this guy called Berend, and me. It's a pretty boring story. So was the girl, actually. She studied philosophy too. First she went out with Herman Mütsel and then with Berend. Never with me. All I ever got to do was listen to her whine. Man – that girl could whine. I was like her Wailing Wall, and do you know how many hours a day the Wailing Wall is open? Twenty-four. Google it. And she knew it too. About Herman, she'd say: 'He thinks the clitoris is like a button, but it's *not*.' And about Berend, she'd go on about how she really saw him as more of a best friend. God, what a boring, whiny girl.

One time she came over for dinner and made me a delicious shakshuka. I must admit that sometimes incredibly boring girls can make really delicious meals, like shakshuka, for example. After dinner she had to pee, and when she came back from the bathroom she stood in the middle of my room and said, 'Sofie, I hope this won't change our relationship.' When people say things like that, they're usually about to do something that will change the relationship forever.

'Did you think I was into women?' she asked. I told her that such general questions are better reserved for more general occasions. I usually end up saying something strange like that when I don't know what to say. Then she proceeded to make an incredible number of boring statements, mostly about her feelings. To be honest, I have a pretty low tolerance for people and their feelings. Believe it or not, I find myself having conversations like these on a *weekly basis*.

Every time I think I'm finally alone with my own thoughts, some girl comes up to me and starts questioning her sexual orientation. Usually, it starts like this: 'Look, I've never *really* been with a girl. What I mean is that I might've kissed a girlfriend once when I was drunk, but . . .' When people start talking like that, my best advice is to run. Just run. They might chase after you for a little while, but chances are they'll eventually find a girlfriend to share a kiss with when they're drunk.

A week later I had all these missed calls from her on my phone. We needed to meet up for coffee, she said. I remember it well. I ordered a cappuccino, and just as I was about to sip the foam, she told me to forget everything she'd said to me that night. And after my first sip of foam, she said, 'I told Berend about it, and we actually had a good laugh.' Can you imagine? They thought the idea that she might be into women was funny. That's one of the reasons I don't laugh so much any more – it's almost always at somebody else's expense.

Not long after that conversation we all went on a study trip abroad to Copenhagen. We were supposed to assemble four hours in advance, but naturally there was this one girl who still managed to just miss the flight. When asked why she was so late, she replied: 'I don't have my life in order.' Berend and I were standing next to her, and, you guessed it, we both fell instantly in love. Berend and I fell in love with the same girl a lot.

The trip lasted eight days, and in all those eight days I said virtually nothing to her. I just couldn't do it in Copenhagen, I couldn't speak. I get anxious in groups, and when that anxiety gets too big, I get this sharp pain in my chest and lose the ability to speak. It's really horrible, to be honest.

On top of that, Berend spent pretty much the entire trip making out with that super-boring girl. Come to think of it, I was completely surrounded by snogging heterosexuals. We slept in bunk beds, and below me was that girl who cursed like a sailor. She had sex the same way she worked on group projects – decisively and without much finesse. On one of the first nights, as I was climbing up to my bed, she grabbed my hand. 'Want to join in?' Not being able to speak doesn't really help in these kinds of situations. But fortunately, her boyfriend turned round and said, 'That's not what I meant by a threesome, Julia.' Straight people can be funny like that. What he meant was, 'A little lesbian action is nice, but this is a little more than a little.' And he was right, of course.

There was another couple in the corner, and I think the only thing that girl said all week was, 'Harder.' I swear, nobody slept a wink in that room. There was one guy who seemed a little lonely, and halfway through the trip I asked him if I could borrow a pair of socks. Fourteen jackets, six pairs of shoes and one or two pairs of underwear – that's how I usually pack.

It's kind of mean, but I actually ended up stealing those socks. He didn't want to lend them to me, because he thought I could buy my own socks. Technically true, but everything in Scandinavia is super expensive. Plus, we had all these group activities, so there was hardly any time to shop. Then we went to Kierkegaard's grave to see if his tombstone trembled. Kierkegaard wrote this famous book called *Fear and Trembling*. All the students thought it was uproarious.

The group activities slowly turned to hell when that guy realized what I'd done. 'You're wearing my socks,' he said. 'Baloney!' I replied. Most likely the rest of the group thought we'd become the best of friends, because this exchange took place about every ten minutes.

On one of the last days, she started talking to me – that girl who didn't have her life in order – Jules was her name. She had incredibly good posture, and I later found out that she had been studying classical ballet for ten years. I'm sensitive to that kind of thing. She'd just turned eighteen, and I'd just turned twenty-one. We both thought we were incredibly grown-up. And she was – some people are just like that at eighteen. Jules was the female equivalent of Matthijs de Ligt. He always walks across the pitch with his shoulders back, too.

That afternoon we went to the beach to play football, and for a little while the sharp pain in my chest went away. I forget a lot when I play football. On top of that, all those namby-pamby philosophers were completely useless on the field, and everyone suddenly wanted me on their team. Suckers. If it had been up to me, it would've been me vs. the entire group.

Jules was on the other team, and I did exactly what Rose used to do to me: tugged on her shirt even when the ball was nowhere near us. It was pretty funny to watch Jules try to play football. Maybe she wasn't the female equivalent of Matthijs de Ligt after all. She just pranced around the field with those insanely straight shoulders of hers, regardless of where the ball was. It was like she was trying to catch a plane or something. I couldn't help but chuckle. Every now and then I would try to fight with her over the ball, but she wouldn't play. Eventually I got annoyed and kicked her a little too hard. And before I knew it, that arsehole Berend was at her side, helping her up. It's weird, but guys always seem to think that girls need help *getting up*.

I spent the last few days in Copenhagen on the toilet. The hostel had about eight of them, so nobody seemed to notice that one was always occupied. In all the time I spent on that toilet, I could have read *Fear and Trembling* multiple times. But the trouble with my anxiety is that once it's settled in, I can't concentrate on anything. So I just sat there, playing games on my phone. I think I set a world record in Tetris during those hours. I'm really good at Tetris, by the way. People often think the best strategy is to use that long line vertically, but it's not. Using it horizontally works way better in the long run.

On the last evening, I went out with the group to a bar. In Denmark, a small beer costs at least six euros, but that night I just didn't care any more. I hoped that if I drank a lot, I'd be able to speak again. That was a huge mistake. After a while, those sharp pains were pulsing through my entire body. And to make matters worse, I got stuck sitting next to Berend, of all people. He asked me how I'd *experienced* the week. At that moment, I actually wished that I could go and find that cursing girl to help me put it into words.

Of course, I knew what he was doing. I used to do the same thing when I was in primary school. I was pretty popular in primary school, because in primary school people judge you based on what you can *do* – play football, in my case. I still curse the day when all that changed. At some point, you start being judged on the most ridiculous things, like whether you can talk about sex or whether you think the idea of Kierkegaard's grave trembling is *actually* funny. I, for one, don't think it's funny at all, but I *can* cross-kick a ball behind my standing leg. That ought to be enough, if you ask me, but on a study trip abroad with the philosophy department it won't get you very far at all. Believe me.

So, he was doing that thing where you seek out someone sitting alone, someone who's always sitting alone, and ask them *how's it going*, purely because it's going so well for you. Well, I'll play along with a lot of things, but not this kind of crap. To be honest, what I wanted to say was that I wanted to die. Partly because there was some truth to it, and partly because I wanted to wipe that smile off his face. Berend apparently had two pastimes, stealing *my* girls and smiling.

On the flight back, I had a huge hangover, which, oddly enough, didn't affect my Tetris performance much at all. I had just reached an incredibly high level when Jules sat down next to me. At first she just watched me for a while, because no matter how beautiful the girl sitting next to me is, I'm not just going to abandon my vertical blocks. They're always there for me when I need them and thus deserve my full attention.

When I finished my game, we listened to her music for a while. I didn't much like it. She had *taste*, you know? Sometimes too much taste can really put me to sleep. Eventually I asked her if we could listen to my iPod. Then I played Lil' Kleine's entire debut album for her. When people ask for it, I'll give them an education.

Just before we landed, she pulled out the earbuds and said, 'I can't tell if you're extremely confident or extremely insecure.' That's Jules – she never says a word too many. I replied that I felt exactly the way Lil' Kleine feels. And she nodded. That's Jules – she understands a statement like that immediately. And then she just nods.

A few weeks after Copenhagen, I had a house party, and of course the first person to show up was Berend. Don't ask me why, but the people I hate the most are usually the first ones I invite. He said he'd brought ketamine, and that it was really fun.

Word has it that I spent the entire party sitting on a chair in the middle of the room with my head pointing at the floor.

What I do remember is a packed house and a lot of people smacking me on the shoulder. I don't think people even notice what their host is doing. There could be a corpse in the middle of the room for all they care, as long as they can raise a glass.

It's all a blur until the moment Fenna started shaking me. 'Hey *dude*,' she said a few times, then, 'There's this chick here for you.' Well, that woke me up. I opened my eyes to see Jules's face right in front of mine. 'I think you need some fresh air,' she said.

I stumbled out after her, and once we were on the street, I let her have it. 'I don't have time for chicks who pretend to like other chicks but in the end just want Berend.' When I'm under the influence, I use the word 'chicks' a lot. It's a stupid word, I know, but I use it all the time. Jules sighed. 'I think you've miscalculated.' That's what I like about Jules: when she's under the influence, her words become more sophisticated, and she says things like 'miscalculated'.

I think we kissed for about an hour. At some point I said, 'I don't think this is ever going to end.' 'Don't you like eternal things?' she replied. And started kissing me again.

Around four o'clock, we went back to my place. The only ones still there were Berend and all the people he'd given ketamine to. I'm pretty sure there was something wrong with that stuff, because none of those people were doing very well. There was a gigantic man with purple patent leather shoes on my bed. All you could see of him were his shoes, because there were a bunch of girls lying on his back and lower legs having an animated conversation.

What startled me most was seeing this guy I definitely didn't invite but recognized from De Trut. He had a strong Russian accent and was constantly trying to pick up girls at the bar. 'De Trut is for homosexuals, Oleg,' I'd sometimes say to him, but he wouldn't hear it. 'I don't have any homosexuals!' he'd stammer. 'Nobody *has* homosexuals, Oleg,' we tried to explain. But even insights like that weren't appreciated.

Oleg was sitting in the same chair that I'd sat in for hours. And you know what he was doing? Whimpering. Not human whimpering, more like a cat. The sound was deafening. 'Meeooow, meeooowww,' and he held his fingers up like claws. Then this super-skinny girl who was always saying 'I don't *have* a cocaine problem' looked nervously at me and Jules and yelled, 'Can somebody get that guy out of here? *For the love of God*, can somebody get that guy out of here?'

I replied that all cats were welcome at my party and that come to think of it, I wasn't sure why I'd bothered to invite humans. At that, she stormed out the door. I sat down on a chair next to Oleg and let him scratch me a few times. I thought it was kind of cosy, actually. After making out with a girl like Jules, things don't really bother me any more.

But then, out of the corner of my eye, I saw Berend leaning over to whisper something in Jules's ear. Well, it annoyed the hell out of me, so I took it out on the girls on that guy's back. 'You do realize you're sitting on top of someone?' I snapped. 'Yeah, we know. That's Henk, such a sweetie,' they said. 'Ah,' I said. 'Shall we check and see if sweet Henk is still breathing?'

Sweet Henk gave lectures on Bertrand Russell, a philosopher so soporific that I hoped we could list that as the cause of death. After we turned him over, no one dared go near his mouth. It's kind of cruel of me to say this, but sweet Henk already looked like he was beginning to waste away. In the end, we decided to splash some water in his face. He woke up, thank God, and thanked me for the party. 'Oh, my pleasure,' I said and showed him to the door.

The next thing I did was tell those girls to fuck off. It's weird, but when something's really bothering me, I attack all kinds of other things rather than the problem itself. Sometimes I never even get round to the problem itself. This probably has to do with the fact that I'm cut from IKEA wood.

Other than Berend and Jules, the only person left at the party was Oleg. I stood by him for a while and pawed him back every now and then, but honestly, I'd had enough. I asked him to knock it off, and he started meowing even louder. Well, as you can imagine, I was sinking into despair. Fifteen minutes later, Berend came up to me and said, '*We're* going to head out.' My god, that guy. I could've strangled him.

Later, Jules and I dated for a while, but I broke it off after a few months. When Berend heard that Jules was on the market again, he dumped that super-boring girl he was seeing. I'm pretty sure that he and Jules still have a thing. I don't need to know, to be honest. I hope they're wildly unhappy together. I broke up with Jules because I couldn't handle someone getting close to me. Whenever I have an immediate click with somebody, it stops being fun. Weird, I know.

Jules would always say, 'It feels as if you have one eye on me and one eye on the rest of the world.' She meant it as criticism, but I thought it sounded logical. Imagine navigating traffic with both eyes on her the whole time – it would be a disaster. But I kind of get it. People in love are usually seeking confirmation. I'm not so good at that. I like buying people ice cream and bigger gifts too – but confirmation? Anything but that.

My philosophy studies only got one eye as well. Every six months we had an evaluation with our mentor, who always said there was a career in academia for me if I stuck with it. Thanks, but no thanks, sir. A couple of meetings with white people about the curriculum, and before long they're cutting your funding because you can't churn out a new paper every week. Do you know how many people actually read the average philosophical paper? Zero-point-four. Zero-point-four people! That means that the paper you slaved over for months will only ever be read by someone's lower legs. I think I'll pass.

So the next time my mentor told me to stick with it, I said, in the words of J. Cole, who's almost as good a rapper as Lil' Kleine, 'I got a date with destiny, I'm running late for that.' That's what I said to the guy. He dropped his head on the table and said: 'Yes, Sofie, we all know you want to be famous.' I'd often correct him by saying that it was recognition I wanted, not fame. That's what everyone who wants to be famous says. Sometimes I'd also add that just because *he* never became a celebrated writer, it didn't mean I wouldn't either. It's a wonder the man agreed to sit down and talk with me every six months.

During my final evaluation session, I could barely stand

because I'd drunk so much the night before, trying to muster enough courage to kiss Georgina Verbaan, the famous actress who happened to be at Paradiso that night. Let's just say that I more or less succeeded. You're probably wondering how that's possible – how do you more or less kiss somebody? Well, here's what happened: I saw her in the club and asked her if she wanted a drink. Or actually it went more like this: a girl I knew from before came up to me earlier in the night to say what a pity it was that I'd cut off all my hair and started dressing like a man. She said I used to be so much prettier. The comment made me want to cry and kill everybody. When I'm sad, I often get this feeling like I want to kill everybody.

It's funny actually – that girl worked for an organization that promoted the rights of the LGBTQIA+ community. Now I can't help but wonder what this organization actually did and which department she worked in. 'Eradication from Within', probably. Anyway, I went off in tears to the bar, where I asked if I could just have everything; the bartender said, 'No beer for you yet, not until you're sixteen, bro.' One thing I've noticed is that guys are always so *nice* to each other. Whether you're fifteen or thirty-four, you're always somebody's *bro*, which is why I didn't dare reveal that I was a woman – I'd lose a whole group of friends. And what a group it was.

My brother was at Paradiso that night too, and he had a beard. When you have a beard, people give you everything. You really can't go wrong. As soon as he saw my face, he ordered six beers for me. 'Now get lost,' said the bartender with a wink.

I'm telling you: men – they know how to have a great time together.

I chugged the first few beers myself and took the last two over to Georgina Verbaan. I think she was stunned when she saw me. My eyes stay red for a long time after crying. 'Wanna beer?' I asked. She held up the fullest beer in the history of draft beers. I sighed and shot a hostile look at the guy she was talking to. He probably thought I was her long-lost son or something and wondered whether he should make a run for it.

Maybe she thought I was her son too. 'How old are you anyway?' she asked. You know what I said? I mentioned my brother's date of birth and proceeded to explain that *his* mother was not *my* mother, but we did have the same father. It's really not that complicated, but when you explain it quickly people easily get confused. And when people get confused, they lose interest in your exact age. And you know what's ironic? I was actually in my early twenties when this happened. But when everybody just assumes you're fifteen, you start to believe it yourself.

Georgina Verbaan truly is a nice person. I don't care what you think of her, you probably don't even know her. I do know her: I know where she buys her groceries and what kinds of things she eats for breakfast. I asked her all these things and she answered very politely. While we were talking, a couple of guys walked by and gave me a thumbs-up. That kind of thing gets old after a while. I wanted them to stop, so I took a very deep bow. Like really deep. All the way to the ground. Naturally, Georgina Verbaan was not amused and walked away. But half an hour later I bumped into her again on the dance floor and she started telling me again where she buys her groceries – at Marqt with a q. Here's a little tip for anyone who wants to strike up a conversation with Georgina Verbaan: just start talking about Marqt with a q. She could go on about it for hours.

Eventually it was closing time, and I lost sight of her. I searched for her like a man possessed. I can be really passionate at moments like that. Plus, I was wearing my lucky Decathlon shirt – things just have a way of working out in that shirt. I was wearing it the first time I kissed Jules, and it's been my lucky shirt ever since. It's got a big Nike swoosh on it. Nobody knows what the swoosh means, but I do: it means that if I want to make out with Georgina Verbaan, I should go for it.

I couldn't find her inside, so I checked outside. It was early November and freezing cold. With chattering teeth, I pushed my way through the crowd, occasionally tapping the shoulder of a woman who looked like her. Finally I found her. She was standing outside the bike garage. I told her I'd probably catch pneumonia if I stood there a minute longer. She nodded. 'You were the most pleasant woman I spoke to all evening,' I said, and it was true. 'And you were the most beautiful,' she replied.

Well, that gave me the confidence I needed. I kissed her on the lips, and she kissed me back. Four seconds of pure bliss. When I say that I more or less kissed her, what I mean is that when people think of kissing they often imagine a lot of tongue. Now, I've got a lot of nerve, but not *that* much nerve. I'm not going to kiss Georgina Verbaan in the freezing cold and then try to open my mouth too. I wouldn't dare. Not even in my Decathlon shirt.

All of this is to say that during that meeting with my mentor, I was completely ecstatic. I sat down at the table in a beer-sloshed stupor. And in case you haven't noticed, I can be kind of macho sometimes. Machos like to brag about all the women they've slept with, and when Georgina Verbaan has recently joined the ranks, they're obviously not going to leave that unsaid. So I shouted, 'Georgina Verbaan, Thomas, Georgina Verbaan!' My mentor's name was Thomas. His head hit the table relatively early that morning.

That pissed me off somewhat. What I wanted to say was, 'Just because *you've* never kissed Georgina Verbaan for four seconds doesn't mean . . .' Jerk. People are always condescending about things that are out of their own reach. And just when it seemed like I was done, I got riled again. 'Georgina! Thomas! Georgina! It doesn't get any better than that!' He looked at me long and hard and said, 'Sofie, believe me, it *will* get better.' Total nonsense, I'm telling you.

My Pretty Little Sofie

Believe it or not, for a while there I was throwing up everything I ate. Idiotic, I know. I would advise everyone to keep as much of their food down as possible. Throwing up all your food will make you utterly miserable if you do it for long enough. Every time I bent over the toilet, there were these two cats who would come and sit beside me, which is why I finally stopped. Sometimes, when you really don't have your best interests at heart, you need someone there who does. Their presence forces you to pull yourself together, whether you want to or not.

So in my case it was the cats that did it. In a way they saved my life. You know what it was? I actually wanted to set a good example for them. I wanted those cats to know that it doesn't matter what people say, whether about your fur or your figure in a broader sense. Screw them – that's what I wanted those cats to know. *Screw them.*

Every time I knelt down, one cat would sit on the left of the toilet and the other on the right. They'd stare at me intently, as cats sometimes do. It's the same look I get on my face when I'm doing my tax return, but without the panic. I didn't know what to say to them at those moments. There's really no logical justification for throwing up your food when you think about it.

After a while, I realized that maybe that's what they were trying to tell me: that what I was doing was ridiculous, and also fairly objectionable. If cats were language teachers, I think they'd use expressions like 'fairly objectionable' all the time. That's how cats are.

Those cats were filthy rich by the way, living in Oud-Zuid. They ate nothing but Royal Canin, the most expensive cat food ever, and turned their noses up at everything else. To be honest, I understood where they were coming from. I had a cat of my own for a while. His name was Bassie. He ate literally everything, and things didn't end well for him. Bassie was extremely charismatic, but he had a penchant for the darker side of life. After a few months, we had to mix anti-depressants into his food. People in Oud-Zuid do that kind of thing. But in the end, there was no saving him. Sometimes housemates just can't be saved. He was like a fat orange Amy Winehouse.

The thing about Bassie was that he never landed on his feet when he fell. He just thundered down the stairs. At one point, I even suspected that he was doing it on purpose, because the women at the vet went wild when he came in. Like I said, he was quite the charmer. He took any belly rub he could get.

But God, what a stinker. We really should've taken out some kind of nine-lives insurance on him, because that was the only cat cliché that actually applied to him. Bassie definitely had multiple lives, and when I look back on his eventful existence, I wonder if he might have had one too many.

The cats with me in the bathroom were only there because I was cat-sitting. We never really got to know each other. They just saw me through my worst. I can't really explain where the vomiting came from, and maybe it doesn't matter. People always think you throw up your food because you want to be skinny. Personally, I think that if you're throwing up your food, you mostly just want to throw up your food. You want to come as close to death as possible without actually dying. Because once you're dead, you won't have any cats staring at you. When you throw up your food, you value life just enough to appreciate something like that.

I looked after those cats for a whole summer. When I wasn't with them, I was working at Café in the City. If I were you, I'd avoid that place at all costs. Everything on the menu was gross and expensive, and if you asked where your food was, you had to deal with Joe. Joe was a guy you didn't want to deal with. Whenever the servers came back with a complaint, he had just one question: Are they locals or are they *tourists*? I found the question almost touching. I don't think a local had set foot in that place since the 1980s. The customers were *always* bloody tourists. If they kept asking about the whereabouts of their fried egg, Joe would tell me to tell them it was up their arse. That's what I was supposed to tell them. I had long blonde hair back then, and when you have long blonde hair, you can say the most shocking things about eggs and people will just keep ogling you.

When Joe wasn't at work, he was at home in the suburbs, where he had multiple screens set up so he could still keep an eye on things at the café. Actually, I was more afraid of Joe when he wasn't there than when he was. He was always calling to tell me to stop fiddling with my hair. In my early days at Café in the City, I'd have to listen to a whole lecture about hair fiddling, but after a while he'd just call and say, 'Hands off!' and then hang up. It really stressed me out. And, believe it or not, when I'm stressed, I fiddle with my hair.

My favourite co-worker at Café in the City was Bennie, and he always wore purple. I thought it was sweet. He was a server like me, and every time we looked out over a terrace full of ranting tourists, he'd whisper, 'God, I really want to have a threesome, Sof.' And I'd nod. Usually men say that when they want a threesome with you, but Bennie wasn't like that. He'd always follow up with, 'But I'm just not ready yet, Sof, I'm not ready yet.' I thought that was sweet too. For Bennie, a threesome was the most sacred thing one could have. Some people hope to earn an honorary doctorate or see Feyenoord win the national championships, but Bennie just hoped for a threesome. I like that – I like people who believe in something sacred.

It was also funny how Bennie was constantly fretting over his future threesome. Whenever I asked him a more technical question about it, he'd panic. 'How are you going to divide your attention?' I'd ask. 'No idea, Sof, no idea!' If I kept going on in that vein, the customers stopped getting their food altogether. But after you've worked at Café in the City for long enough, you really couldn't care less. You're more concerned about getting through the day without too many calls from Joe. And without anybody getting their teeth knocked out. That happened sometimes.

Oddly enough, it always happened to the same guy. About once a week, I'd come into work and hear someone say, 'Joel got another tooth knocked out.' Don't ask me why, but Joe named his son Joel. Joel was pretty much the only person at Café in the City who would do more than just shrug if the entire place went up in flames. He actually *cared* about the business. He really shouldn't have if you ask me. Caring about a place like Café in the City is kind of like caring about Katy Perry. There are some things you really shouldn't bother with.

But since Joel actually cared about the business, he'd always run after tourists who left without paying. There were a few times when he even chased them on to the tram. I can tell you for a fact that Line 1's service was temporarily suspended because Joel was chasing some couple down the aisle. But even though Joel was fast, he wasn't very strong. This meant that he usually had a big problem when he finally came face to face with the culprits.

After work, all the employees at Café in the City would hang out and drink a shitload of beer. You know what I did? I would *order* a beer and then walk around with it for a while without taking a sip. After twenty minutes, I'd go into the bathroom and empty the glass. I did this because there are a ton of empty calories in beer. Empty calories are calories that don't offer any long-term sustenance.

Oatmeal, on the other hand, is what they call a nutrient-dense food, full of *non*-empty calories. Which is why I started eating only oatmeal. Oatmeal for breakfast; oatmeal for lunch; and sometimes even oatmeal for *dinner*. I can't eat oatmeal any more. If you eat enough of it, you just can't get it down any more. Especially after you've seen it come back *out*.

You know what the thing is? You have to throw up your food as soon as possible after you eat, so that your body doesn't have time to absorb it. But that's not the kind of tip I want to give you here. I really do have your best interests at heart, and it is my fervent wish that all the food you eat be absorbed by your body. Please, don't throw up your food. It won't get you anywhere in life, except maybe in your own head. That's why people do it, I think. Because the world is just too damn big, and we're desperate for *boundaries*. When all you eat is oatmeal, your world becomes very small. You can touch the sides, which is why people do stuff like that – because we long for touch, and sometimes you can't find anyone who can offer you that.

My world *was* too big that summer. It was the summer before I started studying Russian, and it's crazy, but I was hardly speaking to anyone at that point. I spent a lot of time thinking about Douchebag D. I thought about him, and about how he was the only one who knew how to close those doors and windows and say, 'Okay, that's enough now' – with him, I actually dared to believe it. Sometimes you really want to call a person like that but can't because he called you a lesbian fundamentalist.

I think the only person I talked to that entire summer was Bennie, and a little bit to the cats. And that's how it starts. You get these voices in your head that tell you that kneeling in front of the toilet is actually going to solve something. What exactly needs solving, you can't quite say. All you know is that if you become fragile enough they might get scared. They have to get scared, you think, because if they get scared they might come back. Who 'they' are you can't quite say, they're just – people who know how to close the goddamn doors and windows.

The reason I wanted to study Russian was that I wanted to be a translator. It sounded like an amazing profession. What I didn't know then was that translators are actually *really* badly paid. There are only a few things in this world that truly *infuriate* me, and translator pay is one of them. You know what it is? Translators believe in something sacred, and if you ask me, people like that ought to be paid properly.

There were three Russian teachers: Elizaveta, Czarina and Natasha. Elizaveta was the only one you could pull a fast one on. She was pretty jaded. She just said, '*Privyet*,' and then sank back into her chair. Then we were just supposed to start making conversation in Russian. Well, this is pretty much impossible when you're just starting out with the language – especially when you haven't even learned the alphabet yet. I'm pretty sure Elizaveta believed that the Netherlands had once been part of the Soviet Union, and that we only spoke Dutch out of pride.

Natasha was another story. She hated us from the bottom of her heart, and after a while we knew why. It turned out that Natasha had a bone to pick with the entire Dutch population, and this had to do with a story floating around the internet. Apparently she'd moved to Amsterdam for love, but things didn't end well. How *exactly* they ended, we don't know. What we do know is that her ex-husband wrote more than three thousand words about the chlamydia she gave him. Everything you'd ever want to know about Natasha's chlamydia is online. Personally, I think this is pretty shitty, because with the right treatment chlamydia eventually goes away. For everybody else in this world, there's life after chlamydia, and that life is fairly comfortable. But not for Natasha. Natasha will forever be associated with that *burning* sensation when you pee, and I can certainly understand her desire to see at least one nation pay for that.

We had to pay. Natasha made us memorize all the Russian verbs of motion by heart. That is about the worst punishment imaginable. In Russian, there are fourteen ways to say 'to go'. These are then divided into categories: *spatial, temporal* and *resultative*. And within these categories are several different sub-categories. And if you thought that wasn't enough, Natasha forced us to learn all the different forms of the past tense and the ways that these verbs were conjugated in it. The differences in verb forms can be so subtle, and so different from Dutch, that it's virtually impossible to master them after the age of twelve. Or at least that's what Natasha told us: 'From puberty onwards, this is pretty much impossible.' Well, I don't know if you've ever sat in a lecture hall, but they are generally full of people who've been going through puberty for a *really* long time. Sometimes they're even out of it already.

Since I was post-pubescent by the time I started studying Russian, I decided to speak exclusively in the resultative tense. This is for completed actions that involve moving back and forth in opposing directions. For example: 'I went to Natasha's house without chlamydia and returned home with chlamydia.' If you speak only in the resultative tense, you can't prove that Natasha actually gave you chlamydia – doing so would put you back in the more spatial and temporal zones. But you can *suggest* that she had something to do with it.

Now, you have to understand that Elizaveta, Natasha and we, the students, all belonged to the same camp, and it was a particularly gloomy one. Only a small, determined minority ever managed to see the light, and I'm not sure if I was one of them. As is often the case, the group that continued to the bitter end was made up of people capable of harming themselves before anyone else did.

For the first twenty minutes of Czarina's classes she usually wasn't there. Nevertheless, we all sat silently in the classroom waiting for her to arrive. Like Joe, Czarina was more powerful in her absence. You smelled her before you saw her. The intoxicating scent of her perfume would drift down the hall, and a second later she'd appear – not Czarina, but her purple fur coat. A purple fur coat on click-clacking heels, topped by a strange hairdo that was either red or brown, I could never decide which. That's the thing about people who scare you to death, you never get a good look at them.

Once in the room, she tossed her bag on the desk. Then she was quiet, and we were even quieter. Then she'd laugh and say, '*Umnitsa*,' which means something along the lines of 'Well done'. But we hadn't done anything yet. Then she'd call on someone, preferably the worst student in the class, and ask them to read aloud.

We were always having to memorize texts. We'd practise them ten times with a CD-ROM and ten times without. On the CD, you'd hear a woman pronounce everything extremely clearly. I don't know where they found that lady, but clearly she'd never met Czarina. She sounded way too relaxed for that. You can learn a lot of things from another person – like how to pronounce difficult vowel sounds and insanely long sentence structures – but unfortunately how to calm your mind isn't one of them. You've got to figure that one out on your own.

And that's why we would never sound like that woman on the CD, you know? Not in a million years. Czarina would either let you speak, or she'd interrupt you. If you were really struggling with a word, she'd make you finish. And just when you thought you were on a roll, she'd say '*Lyubov*,' or 'darling'. And once Czarina had called you 'darling', it was up to you to dissociate as quickly as possible. Any sense of self-esteem – or anything that resembled emotion whatsoever – had to be blocked out immediately. You had to get out of there, only without leaving your seat, which is actually extremely hard to do, and God knows how many times we witnessed futile attempts at dissociation.

At the start of the academic year, there were about forty of us. By Christmas, there were only twelve. Twelve – and all absolutely nuts. You had to be if you were going to survive that level of torment day in and day out. But I managed to make two really amazing friends in the Russian department. Two really amazing friends who, once they found out I was into women, never called me again. Their names were Mike and Max. Mike and I spent the entire year talking about nothing but Ajax – Amsterdam's soccer team. I never knew there was so much to say about Ajax until I met Mike.

You know which Ajax player I was really into that season? Lucas Andersen. Lucas Andersen was Danish. I like the Danes. They're like Dutch people who've just spent a little longer under the shower. Dutch people with very expensive conditioner. I can't even imagine how many types of conditioner Lucas Andersen had. He had a beautiful head of hair that swayed in perfect harmony with every move he made on the pitch. Lucas Andersen was an incredibly graceful player – an artist, that's what he was.

Still, he didn't last long on the Ajax team. The guy just didn't move towards the goal. He danced across the field in all his gracefulness, without ever going in any clear direction. I'm easily moved by that kind of thing. But most Ajax fans don't seem to appreciate it. I don't think Ajax fans are familiar with the concept of 'being moved'. Fenna always says, 'People go to the Ajax stadium for emotional housekeeping, and that's probably a good thing.' But I don't know if it's such a good thing. It's like having sex with someone who only cares about the orgasm. They don't give a damn as long as there's some kind of *eruption*.

Well, Lucas Andersen had a lot of things to offer, but eruptions weren't among them. I guess he was kind of lesbian in that way. A lot of foreplay – I mean *a lot* – followed by so many different manoeuvres that you'd forget what he was trying to achieve in the first place. In a way, Lucas Andersen played football the same way I write. I usually forget what I'm trying to achieve too. You're probably starting to wonder about this yourselves. But at least you're *friendlier* about it than most of the people in the stadium, you know? Maybe you're kind of lesbian too.

Mike thought Lucas Andersen was a fag. That's what he used to say: 'I don't have anything against fags, but he's definitely one of them, okay?' It's funny, people like to say they don't have anything against fags or Moroccans or dykes, but they still have to refer to them in those terms. You'd have to hook them up to a respirator if they suddenly weren't allowed to use those words any more. And if you were to call *them* something like that, they'd lose their shit. People are pretty pathetic when you think about it. Actually, the longer you think about it, the more you want to lock them all up. Preferably in drawers.

These are the drawers I'd use: one for people in the Ajax stadium; one for people who start their sentences with 'I have nothing against'; one for people who use the word 'Moroccans' to describe people who have lived in the Netherlands for generations; and one for people who walk up to pairs of lesbians in restaurants and tell them they make a beautiful couple. All of these drawers would be labelled with an ugly-coloured sticker and – call it a violation of human rights – once I'd shut them, I'd never open them again.

Well, actually, you know what I'd do? Every once in a while, on a Sunday afternoon, I would open one and look down at the occupants screaming and shouting and say, 'You've been in this drawer for generations, I think it's time for you to stop playing the victim.' Then I would close it again and calmly go about my afternoon.

If I had it my way, I could've gone a whole day without talking to anyone but Mike, but Max was always there too. It's not nice of me to say, but sometimes that happens in friend groups – that there's one person who's just there. Max was madly in love with me. So was Mike, but he translated all his love into facts about Lucas Andersen and Thulani Serero. Max didn't. Max just offered me his love in its most uncompromised form. He'd been carrying my passport photo around since the first week of class, which is a pretty weird thing to do, and the kind of thing you really ought to nip in the bud if you want to avoid problems down the road. But I like to let problems come to fruition naturally, and even then I don't intervene.

Max wanted to be a poet, and around that time so did I. But he was a lot braver than I was. He basically slept on the doorstep of De Bezige Bij, the chicest literary publisher in

Amsterdam. And whenever somebody cracked the door open for him, even just a tiny bit, he shouted that he had more. A word of advice for people trying to find a publisher: never shout that you have more. They'll deadbolt the door on you. If it were up to publishers, everyone would just stop writing literature. They're up to their eyeballs in literature. If you really want to find a publisher, you're better off saying that you have a refreshing personality. Then they're all ears. After that, the trick is to mention *very* subtly that you might want to write a book someday. Trust me. It worked for me.

The problem with Max was that his personality wasn't exactly refreshing. But it was decisive. One time I went with him to the headquarters of De Bezige Bij, and they actually let him in, albeit very briefly. It was a horrible experience. We were barely in the entrance hall when a woman stormed out to meet us. 'You're on the pile!' she shrieked. What being 'on the pile' really means is that you can forget about it. In the publishing world, 'the pile' is just a fancy word for the trash. But I didn't mention this to Max.

Oddly enough, he didn't leave. He just stood there nodding at the giant fancy floor tiles in the entrance hall, without making any eye contact with her. I think Max thought those tiles were the real employees of De Bezige Bij. Well, then something really outrageous happened. The woman farted. Not a loud one, but a wet, quiet, nasty little fart. I thought about it a lot afterwards, and I think they instructed her to do it: 'If an author gets really persistent – let one rip.'

In the end, I had to tug at Max's sleeve. Otherwise, he'd

probably still be standing there. Nothing would make him leave the room – not even the godawful smell. He just stood there breathing in and out, as if he was the one who had farted. Max became one with De Bezige Bij very early on, I think.

In Czarina's class, the three of us sat in a row. I was always in the middle, with Mike and Max on either side, though that didn't make me feel any safer. Really, we made a mess of things together. For starters, Mike spoke Russian as if it were a language only to be spoken when you were totally wasted at a bar in the Jordaan, or as if folk singer André Hazes had survived his multiple cardiac arrests but couldn't get his vowels and consonants straight any more. Nobody understood a *word* he said. And when Czarina tried to correct him, he would say, 'Yeah, yeah, yeah.' I liked that about Mike. He wasn't afraid of anybody. By the end of the year, he managed to say, '*Da, da, da*' instead, but that was the only noticeable progress he made.

I wonder what he's up to these days. Mike was studying Russian because he wanted to go into business. 'Somebody's got to communicate with those bastards, Sof,' he'd say. And I wholeheartedly agreed with him. He was always talking about Putin. He liked to say that one day he was just going to call him up – 'I'm gonna set that guy straight,' he'd say. I sincerely hope he does. But he'll need to be able to say more than 'da, da, da'. Otherwise, Putin will be the one setting Mike straight.

Nobody could understand Max either. But for a different, more essential reason. Max was a mumbler. It was as if the words never made it out of his mouth. Whenever Max read out loud, all you heard was a sort of low grumble from the corner of the room. Which is why Czarina hated him, because it is impossible to teach someone like that. She'd lash out at him, hurling insults that most students would never recover from – not as students, and not as human beings. How Max dealt with it was a mystery to us: we could barely understand him, even in Dutch.

Max was from the south and spoke with a thick accent. Now, I don't want to speak badly of the people of Brabant, but when you talk like that and direct your speech down at the floor tiles, it can really become a drain on the people around you. In the beginning, we just let him go on for a bit, but eventually, Mike and I had so much Ajax business to discuss that we didn't have time for it any more. Sometimes Mike would just speak over him and say: 'Sof, I swear to God, I don't understand a *word* this guy is saying.' I didn't understand a word Max was saying either. But he was there, you know?

Czarina and I had a complex relationship. Actually, it was about as complex as it can get between women. For starters, she always called me her 'pretty little Sofie'. If you really want to cut off all the oxygen to my head, just call me 'my pretty little Sofie'. Czarina's pretty little Sofie got called on in every class, usually to read the most complicated texts possible. Czarina had come up with a particularly crafty strategy for dealing with me, and let's just say, it worked.

One afternoon, I was reading out loud a text by Daniil Charms, and she interrupted me. She said, '*Lyubov*, I didn't know you had dyslexia.' 'I don't,' I replied, and she allowed me to continue. Thirty seconds later, she interrupted me again and asked, 'Then what cognitive disorder do you have?'

The embarrassing thing about it was that Daniil Charms' work is actually pretty simple. Difficult to write, but not to read. There was a photo of him smoking a cigar next to the text. After her second remark, I just stared down at that cigar. But I had to keep reading, you know? Even with the massive lump in my throat. Then it really sounded like I had dyslexia or some other cognitive disorder. That was the worst thing about Czarina: you had no choice but to accept that she was right.

After class, I remained in my seat and told Mike and Max not to wait for me. When everyone was gone, and it was just me and Czarina, I walked up to her and said, 'This has to stop.' Okay, so you can't always count on me for elegant sentences. When the going gets rough, those sentences say thank you very much and get the hell out of there. Useless is what they are.

Suddenly, I just started bawling. Czarina already had her purple fur coat on, and after repeating '*Moya prikrasnaya devushka*' (my lovely little girl) several times, she took me into her arms. Well, that made me cry even harder, and with passion. When you cry passionately, you cry for everything. I cried for Mike and for Max and for myself, and because I was her pretty little Sofie. *That* really made me cry.

Believe it or not, she started kissing away my tears. Can you imagine? Czarina, in her purple fur coat, kissing the tears from your cheeks. I remember actually wanting to kiss her back, and of course that made me sob even harder. When I sob, my breath gets confused. My entire body started shaking, and Czarina held me even tighter. She said, 'I'll let go when you've calmed down.' We stood there like that for about twenty minutes. Every now and then she'd whisper that I was too beautiful to cry. And I just kept on sobbing because I felt like that wasn't true – you know?

That was the weirdest thing about that time: people kept telling me how *beautiful* I was, when I knew I wasn't. Beauty is strange like that. I write this now with a shaved head and a couple of pimples on my face. And I have no trouble looking at myself this way. But back then, I couldn't – not ever. Back then I always wanted to try and outwit mirrors, because every time I looked into them I saw something that I wasn't, and that's unbearable.

But eventually the mirrors catch up with you. They'll inevitably suck you in, and you'll see yourself for what you are – a little too blonde, a little too thin, a little too fragile. And I promise you – there's only one thing you can say to yourself at such moments: 'It's not your fault, it's not your fault, it's not your fault.' Because it really isn't your fault, it's the fault of all those people who've *never* said it out loud, but who slowly but surely rammed it down your throat.

A month after Czarina held me in her arms, we went to Kaliningrad and Gdańsk. The geniuses in our student association decided that January would be a good time to go, when the wind chill is about thirty below zero. That's cold. I mean like *really* cold. And it's especially cold when all you have is a pair of All Stars and an Ajax scarf with you, like Mike and I did. We believed that a true Ajax fan would always be kept warm by that scarf, but we learned that this isn't necessarily the case.

Mike and I exchanged about three words the entire trip. The rest of the time we walked behind the group, staring at the ground. Every now and then we'd lose them because we didn't have the energy to lift our heads and check where they were going. Besides, when it's minus thirty, it's hard to walk in any specific direction. You just walk. And if you manage to think about anything, you think about your toes. You wonder how many you used to have. Anticipating grief – that's what you're doing. You think about all the experiences you've had with your toes, all the great times, but all the bad times too, and you try to tell yourself to cherish the good memories.

On the second day, Mike gave me a dull look and slowly reached into his pocket. For a few minutes, I just stared at him with the same dazed look in my eyes, until he finally pulled it out – a small flask. 'Drink,' he said in a low, dark tone. To this day, I don't know what was in the bottle, but one sip was enough to burn away half my organs. That might sound unpleasant, but at those temperatures it's surprisingly comforting to know that you still have organs.

That flask stayed with us all across Eastern Europe. How he managed to keep it filled, I have no idea. But under conditions like that, you don't ask questions. If someone says, 'Drink,' you drink. And if one of the tour guides says, 'Walk,' you walk. If you've ever harboured a secret desire to be a cow, I strongly recommend a study-abroad trip to Gdańsk and Kaliningrad.

I couldn't help but feel sorry for Mike – he caught a lot more wind than I did. Mike was really tall, like a tree. In Gdańsk, he behaved like a tree, too. If you didn't order him to walk in a certain direction, he just stood there with his shaved head towering over everyone. He stared out at all the people and then back down at the pavement. It made me sad to look at him. At moments like that, you forgot that he had nothing against fags. You just wanted to take him in your arms and read him a sweet little Toon Tellegen talking-animals book.

Max, on the other hand, was in high spirits the entire trip. 'This is just like working in the *oliebollen* stand,' he kept saying. Max's parents had a stand in Brabant where they sold the sweet, doughy balls during the holidays. He had to work there every winter, and you know what's funny? Max didn't even *like oliebollen*. I get why he was so happy to be in Gdańsk. Nobody in Gdańsk was thinking about sticky, greasy dough-nut balls. As far as I could tell, the people of Gdańsk thought about nothing but Schopenhauer and believing the worst was yet to come.

The evening before we left for Kaliningrad, the three of us discovered the Gdańsk nightlife. We went to at least five bars, and it was in the last one that Mike suddenly wandered off. He walked to the middle of the bar and bent his knees deeply. For those who are not familiar with the Hopak, it's a traditional Ukrainian Cossack dance that dates back to the Middle Ages. It's known for lots of high jumps with the arms and legs spread wide.

Well, things went okay for about half a minute. Mike literally *thundered* around the room, with no regard whatsoever for chairs or bystanders. It was truly breathtaking, but also terrifying: everyone in the bar was watching him until the owner threw a glass at his head. *Everything* is a sensitive subject in Poland, including the Cossack dance.

The glass skimmed his face, and that's when Max and I made a break for it. But not Mike. Mike stayed behind. He wasn't scared of anybody. From out on the street, we heard him bellowing the words of the Ajax fight song: 'You're all just a bunch of *fuuuuuucking* cockroaches!' Of all the Ajax fans, Mike was truly the greatest. Even in a country where people had never even *heard* of Ajax, let alone their arch-rival Feyenoord, he still kept up the fight.

By the time we got to Kaliningrad, all three of us were sick, and so we spent the first few days in the hostel. It had been even colder than we thought during our night out in Gdańsk, but we hardly noticed because of all the vodka. Mike and I played cards, and Max read *Oblomov*. That was when Mike started calling Max 'Bloffo'. 'Bloffo, call Uber Eats,' he would say to him. There was no Uber Eats in Kaliningrad at the time, but Mike found the idea of it calming. So once a day Max had to walk out of the room and pretend to be calling Uber Eats.

The first time we ventured out with the rest of the group, we nearly collapsed. The icy wind cut even deeper into our skin than it had done in Gdańsk. This was probably due to the fact that there are only a handful of buildings in Kaliningrad. Don't ask me why. And the few buildings that were there all seemed to be marked with the wrong opening hours. Every time we tried to go to a museum, it was either temporarily or permanently closed. And that was if you were lucky. If you were unlucky, the museum never existed in the first place. Well, that really made you feel like an idiot – minus thirty-seven degrees, and you find yourself standing in front of a building that doesn't even contain what you were looking for. You could almost feel the building trying not to laugh.

That first day we actually didn't go to a museum at all. You know what we did? We went for a walk. Just to get some fresh air. Can you imagine? After half an hour, one girl started crying. We all felt her pain, but at times like that, you just keep walking. The girl kept walking too, but the crying continued. It's a strange sight – crying people who don't stop walking but just keep walking as they cry. The only thing that stopped were the tears streaming down her face – they literally *froze* to her cheeks. It was actually pretty funny when you stopped to think about it. But you didn't stop, not at thirty-seven below.

It was a disastrous afternoon. Halfway through the walk, we heard somebody shout, 'Bloffooo!' The next moment we saw Max lying face down in the snow. Mike had been sipping his flask all afternoon and had just thrown a giant snowball at Max's head. But the scary thing was – Max didn't get up. He just lay there while Mike yelled, 'Bloffooo! Brabaaant! Hard cock soft g!' 'Hard cock soft g' was another one of Mike's nicknames for Max – a jab at the way people from Brabant pronounce their g's. But all of a sudden it wasn't so funny any more.

A few more people started crying, which I found a bit irritating to be honest. Slavic language students – they're all a bunch of soft-boiled eggs. They can't even take a snowball. I shook Max for a whole minute and screamed for somebody to get Mike under control. But nobody did, they were all way too soft-boiled for that. So Mike just kept shouting from the top of the hill he was standing on, and suddenly Max woke up. Do you know what he said? '*As ge goit, kriedum vaneiges terug in ou gezeecht.*' We've consulted with a number of translators on that one, and apparently it meant something like: 'Don't pitch it if you can't take it.' An incredibly strong comeback from Max, if you ask me. I actually forgot how cold it was for a second when I saw the fire in his eyes.

Then Max ran up the hill and punched Mike in the face. In a way, he didn't fully live up to the expression. Strictly speaking, he should have pitched a snowball back. But maybe the expression is open to multiple interpretations. You can never fully trust a translator. That's because they're severely underpaid. People who are severely underpaid are bound to go rogue after a while.

We went out to a club on our last night in Kaliningrad. The whole group went, which generally isn't a good idea if you actually hope to get in. On top of that, we all looked pretty rough. You know what we looked like? Like we had just crossed the Alps. 'Hannibal + 20' – that's probably what they wrote on the guest list – and Mike was definitely Hannibal. A large portion of his face was green from where Max hit him with his ice-cold fist.

Once we were inside, it turned out that we were the only people there. The crying girl immediately started making out with Max. Nobody saw that coming, not even Max. His eyes were open the whole time they were kissing, and you could just tell they were searching for the tiles on that fancy publisher's floor. He looked a bit lost, and there was absolutely nothing we could do to save him, that was the sad thing about it.

I spent most of the evening on a couch with Mike. Eventually, a group of guys came in, all of them bald. They nodded at Mike because he was bald too. Over the course of the evening, Mike gradually inched closer to me. I noticed this but didn't dare to say anything. I mean, there was nothing wrong with that inching, but after a while you start to wonder what a person is inching towards, you know what I mean?

The group of bald guys got up to leave and each one gave Mike one last nod, and that's when it happened: he leaned towards me and opened his mouth. But what was funny was we were still sitting a little too far apart. If you want to kiss someone, you should really keep your mouth closed until your lips have made contact. Then you've got to commit, otherwise you'll be stuck with a half-baked anecdote for the rest of your life like I had with Georgina Verbaan.

I looked straight into his mouth and saw the tongue that had told me so much about Ajax. What I actually wanted to say was, 'You, tongue, tell me more about Ajax.' But at that particular moment, that tongue wanted something else. That's the thing, if you leave a tongue hanging for too long in a situation like that, it will no longer be willing to speak to you about Ajax or Lucas Andersen.

He turned away from me and pointed at Max. 'You should see Bloffo,' he said. 'Hard cock soft g!' I replied. 'That's my joke,' he snapped. That's what happens. Leave a person's tongue hanging for too long, and they can get really touchy about which jokes are yours and which are theirs. That's how it starts. After a while, they stop calling you altogether.

Manic Pixie Dream Girl

It's possible that some of you are having a hard time following the chronology of my story at this point, which is super annoying, I imagine. So, let me just explain it: the first part of the book is in chronological order; the second part goes back in time. And I'll warn you now, the third part makes a giant leap into something I guess you could call the present. There might have been a more logical way to structure this, but honestly, I've never seen the value of clarity and logic.

What I've been *trying* to do in Part Two is offer some kind of intellectual history, but it's not working. It's important to be transparent about your failures. The reason it's not working is that I keep straying from the intellectual to the sexual. In that sense, I'm a lot more like Sigmund Freud than I thought.

You saw what happened: I *tried* to start with Wittgenstein but ended up with Georgina Verbaan. It happens every time; I can't help it. Besides, I strongly believe that a story tells itself while the author stands by sulking. That's what you learn in literature classes. I majored in literature for a little while there too. In literature classes, you mostly learned one thing: the Author is dead. Technically this is true: most of the writers we read had been dead for an incredibly long time.

It took me a while to understand that the teachers actually meant something else. You know what they meant? They meant that you have to examine the text *itself* and disregard the author's intentions. Pretty insulting if you ask me. I'd be suspicious of anyone who disregarded my intentions. Maybe I'm the first real, living author. If this book is ever discussed in a literary studies seminar, give me a call. I'll bike over and explain to you what my intentions were.

In the literary studies programme, you were required to speak English, because not only did they believe that the Author was dead, they also believed that the entire Dutch language was dead. And as if that wasn't bad enough, everybody used the word 'rather' all the time. I think the students thought that as long as they used that word, whatever they were saying would sound right. *Rather untrue*, if you ask me.

Most of the literature students were kind of dumb. Dumb and undisciplined – two qualities that tend to go together. Literature was a perfect subject for dumb, undisciplined people, because when it came down to it, you could basically say whatever you wanted. Anything is possible once the Author has been declared dead. Whatever you say comes down to a matter of *interpretation*.

After a while, all that interpreting started to drive me

insane. Especially all the nodding that came afterwards. You always had to nod after someone offered their interpretation. It would've been more fun to throw your book at their head. I used to have a football coach who, whenever you missed a goal, would shout, 'Why don't you go and play tennis, man.' That, too, would have been more fun. A teacher who told you to go and play tennis whenever you brought up the topic of Mrs Dalloway's flowers.

I got pretty burned out on *Mrs Dalloway*. *Mrs Dalloway* is the story of a normal day in the banal life of Mrs Dalloway. Well, you've already lost me. Personally, I'd rather read about somebody with an interesting life. On top of that, I had trouble focusing because I was reading from my grandmother's edition, and she wouldn't let me take it out of the house. 'Socks and books – you never get them back,' she said, and she was entirely right about that.

My grandmother was, as my mother liked to put it, 'floating'. And it was true. Most of the time she didn't answer the door when I came by. If I entered with my own key, she'd tap me on the shoulder and say, 'Child, why don't you come back later at a more *Christian* hour?' And that was at three o'clock in the afternoon. My grandmother was always referring to Christian hours, which was ironic given that she had a habit of calling my parents at one thirty in the morning to ask where Tijn was. Tijn is my uncle who's lived up north in Friesland for more than forty years. My mother would tell her exactly that, but she didn't believe it. 'That rascal is probably down at the bar again,' she'd say.

Every time I tried to focus all my attention on the banal life of Mrs Dalloway, my grandmother would ask me who the handsome man on the wall was. 'That was *your* husband,' I'd say. God, that really made her smile, and that warmed my heart. Then she'd go back to bed, surrounded by all her Italian books. My grandmother didn't speak a word of Italian, but she had always considered it a beautiful language. That warmed my heart too.

Since my grandmother warmed my heart, I often stayed the whole afternoon. We would order takeaway. I'm pretty sure that together we ate all the takeaway in the world. She'd always wink at me while we were eating. She was quite the charmer. Sometimes she'd stop abruptly and say, 'Isn't it *absurd* that we're eating babi panggang so early in the morning?' 'It is,' I'd say. And we'd continue our meal.

By the way, we really shouldn't spend too much time talking about *Mrs Dalloway*. I'm a little embarrassed to admit it, but I don't remember very much about it. That happens a lot with books I'm supposed to have an opinion about or see the symbolism in. It's the same reason I don't watch football with guys any more: they always have an opinion about it, and if you keep asking questions, they'll eventually get all symbolic about it.

I've never really understood that kind of thing, not in football and not in literature. For me, whether it's a through pass or a sentence fragment, something has to *happen* for you to actually appreciate it. And the great thing is that there's really nothing to say about it afterwards. I mean, that opening goal by Van Persie against Spain – what can you even say? It just *happened*. Whether you saw it or not.

My god, that goal. I was having pizza with Mike when I saw it, and for reasons I can't explain I threw my pizza out the window. That's how happy I was. Pizzas fall very slowly, by the way. I saw it floating through the air, kind of like Van Persie, and just before it hit the ground it was intercepted by a chair. Imagine that! My neighbours were so happy they threw a chair out the window. If you ask me, that says a lot more than some kind of literary interpretation.

My grandmother eventually died in a nursing home surrounded by a lot of other people who were floating too. It was a house for the floating, located in Amsterdam Nieuw-West. Since the photo of my grandfather always made her smile, we had it hung over her bed. The second time I visited her, she pointed to it again. 'Who's that man with the Jewish schnozz?' she asked. That's when I really understood what my mum meant by floating. I've thought about it a lot since, and the only things that should be allowed to float are Robin van Persie and pizza. They're the only things that are any good at it. With anyone or anything else, it's just hard to watch.

Because everyone in my literature classes kept saying 'rather', I always sat rather close to the door. Get in, get out, I thought. Plus, my English is really bad. Whenever the teacher called on me, I usually limited my response to 'Yes, indeed' or just, 'Indeed.' I put on the best possible British accent I could muster, because speaking with a British accent means you must be well read. Unfortunately, it didn't really work because all the questions were open-ended.

Usually, it went like this: 'Sofie, what are your thoughts on the use of metaphor in the second chapter of Coetzee's *Waiting for the Barbarians*?' 'Yes, indeed.' 'Yes, indeed?' 'Yes, yes, yes, indeed.' Then I'd shoot an aggressive look across the room that said, 'Or maybe somebody else in here would like to try to embody the Dead Author?' After that they leave you alone.

Most of the literature students would piss their pants when they saw me. But I did make one friend – the very girl I was trying to avoid. She was very attractive, and I'm not really into people like that. You know what the problem is with attractive people? They're always so *nice*. Not because they really are nice, but because they're afraid that otherwise people will assume they're not – because they're so attractive. That's one of the main problems with very attractive people. I've thought about attractive people a lot, and the longer you think about them, the more irritating they become.

Frida was *extremely* attractive. So attractive that it took the fun out of it for everybody. So attractive that you wanted to behead anyone standing next to her because they detracted from her beauty. Frida was truly a sight to behold, and if anyone was driven crazy by that, it was her. Actually, I have very little desire to describe her here. I'm sure you can conjure up your own image of such a disgustingly attractive person, so I won't bother.

Well, one day she started whispering things in my ear. And not just any things, lovey-dovey things. In class, we had to listen to the song 'Wild is the Wind' by Nina Simone. It's a song about love – *fierce* love. Now, it's important to understand that all of this happened before I went to De Trut and saw Fenna sitting exhausted on that chair. At that point in my life, I didn't know the first thing about love, let alone the fierce kind. All I knew was how it felt to have some creep pinch your calves and have to put up with it because he was terribly famous. But that's not love, you know?

While the song was playing, she leaned over and whispered that she had given it some thought and decided that she liked 'I Kissed a Girl' by Katy Perry better, that it touched her on a deeper level. That was the worst thing about it – *on top of everything*, she had a sense of humour. Granted, this may not have been her best joke, but she really was funny. That day, it all started to dawn on me. I can't even tell you how exactly it started, you know? That's the thing about fierce love: suddenly, you can only think in *colours*, blissful colours.

It was on a tiny island in the North Sea that I first realized that something wasn't quite right. Believe it or not, the literature department held its introductory camp on Schiermonnikoog. To this day, I have no idea why people go to the Dutch islands for fun. For those who've never been there, let me tell you – it's extremely windy, and there is literally nothing to do except *go for walks*.

The funny thing is that nobody got to know each other at that camp. We only got to know one guy, Dennis. Dennis was in his third year and came along as a counsellor. He spent the whole weekend telling us about the time he had sex with this girl in The Hague and she shat all over him. It was a pretty good story – don't get me wrong. They had gone back to her place, and she insisted on having anal sex. Well, something went wrong, and she pooped. Actually, it wasn't that great a story, now that I think about it. There was no real build-up. But he told it really well.

Halfway through the terrifying ferry trip to the island, Frida discovered that she had forgotten her wallet. I was standing against the railing at the time, thinking about whether or not I should jump. My anxiety was through the roof around this time. When those sharp pangs in your chest get bad enough, you come up with the most frantic ideas to make them disappear. So frantic that you forget that you would disappear with them. You can talk yourself into some pretty silly things if the anxiety gets bad enough. But while I was standing there, Frida started shaking me.

Do you know what I did when she told me that she had left her wallet at home? I gave her mine. 'Here you go,' I said. Can you imagine? I just didn't care any more. Later, I was able to dissect that gesture and identify it as one of *fierce* love. Be warned: if you ever feel compelled to hand over your debit card to someone and say, 'Here you go,' you're probably madly in love with them and no one can save you.

Of all the people I've known, she touched me the most, and you probably don't completely understand why because all I've told you is how pretty she was and that she sometimes forgot her wallet. Obviously, I look for more in a woman than that. You know what I'm looking for? I'm looking for someone who presses her face so close to mine that I forget what's going on in my head. Love is a kind of suicide, you know? You want to disappear, to disappear so much that all the poison you carry around inside you will finally *dissolve*.

I know this sounds like a somewhat negative formulation, but what I've achieved actually *is* negative. I never *had* her, but she did help me overcome a lot of crap. Frida showed me that there was a world where people weren't trying to become one of the Greats, where they just trusted that time would tell and tried to have a little fun along the way. She never went to the supermarket; instead, she did all her shopping at a little Turkish grocery on Bilderdijkstraat. She selected her vegetables very carefully and cooked them extremely slowly. And it was *always* delicious, you know?

This may seem like a small detail, but it's not. People who cook their vegetables very slowly understand something essential. I've never been able to fully grasp the essential, and after Frida I went right back to buying pre-made salads. But with her, I was able to grasp it for a moment. And maybe that's what Frida made me realize – that I was wrong. Wrong when I sat for weeks, months with my back against the fridge reading books, hoping to discover the contours of my existence. That's what I realized – that you never find those contours, you *feel* them, and only when you let someone get close.

And that's the funny thing, you know? You're always so damn *close* to being right. So close that maybe you can only see it when you shut your eyes, which is something you can't do until you've let go of some of that goddamn fear. I know that all of this sounds like the lyrics to a Top 40 song, but it's true.

It was hard though, because she left again. People often leave without saying goodbye. Which is funny, really. Here's what happened: after every class, I'd ask Frida what she was going to do, and she'd say, 'No idea, what are *you* going to do?' to which I'd reply that, believe it or not, I actually had less of an idea than she did. This is another way to know if your love is fierce: all of a sudden you're already *completely* out of ideas.

After we had established that neither of us knew what we were going to do next, we'd go and sit by the canal. That's what we always did: sit by the canal, where I'd tell jokes until Frida's stomach hurt. That was my ultimate goal – to make Frida yell 'Stop it! My stomach!' And of course, I'd just keep going. That was the best part, seeing Frida sprawled out along the canal, practically rolling on the ground, while I just went *on and on*.

In the meantime, she rolled an incredible number of cigarettes, and occasionally she'd say, 'I actually don't smoke.' 'Oh, me neither,' I'd reply, 'absolutely not,' and then I'd ask her to roll one for me. After an hour or so she'd finally ask the question: 'But how are you really, my sweet?' Well, by then I'd be ready to spill my guts to her. I'd tell her all about the sharp pains in my chest, about whether or not I was able to swallow, about the great mind I would probably never become. And how I didn't really care so much any more, you know?

Then we'd go to the Turkish grocery and back to her place for dinner, and then *my* stomach would start hurting because everything was taking so long. '*Actually,* I really should be getting home,' I'd say after a while. 'I know,' she'd reply, 'but *actually* you can stay over if you want.' Not once did I refuse her invitation, but here's the stupid thing: there wasn't a single night when I didn't feel, at least for a moment, right before falling asleep, that it was all just passing me by. That's without a doubt the worst thing about me: I never *trust* anything. You know what it is with love? You have to trust its whole *movement*. Not just the beginning, not just the end – the whole goddamn movement. But I couldn't.

And if all you ever think about is how it's going to end, the end will inevitably come. I was stupid enough to take Frida to a jazz concert, though I don't even like jazz, and she couldn't take her eyes off the pianist. Can you believe it? The pianist. Since all we ever did was sit by that canal, and the only place we ever went was the Turkish grocery, I thought it would be nice to take her somewhere new. I'm telling you – when you're that lovesick and you finally manage to come up with an idea, it usually has disastrous consequences.

Before I knew it, I was stuck with him: Arthur. Arthur the jazz pianist, a guy who said '*Wowee*, that's awesome' in response to pretty much everything that was said. Pretty soon, Frida was nowhere to be found after class. She had already been picked up by Arthur on his cargo bike. I would've loved to have pushed that red cargo bike straight into the canal. The worst thing about it was that I still stayed with her. Sometimes you just need to back off, but I couldn't.

Soon my days were filled with Arthur, Arthur, Arthur. In Arthur's world, you encountered very few other people. Actually, it was mostly just Arthur. Frida was there too, but to Arthur, she was more of a mirror. When he looked at her, he probably thought – more Arthur! I'm telling you, people who use other people as mirrors are the biggest arseholes of them all.

And that's what makes talking about Frida so complicated. You think you're talking about *her*, but you're really just talking about yourself for the hundredth time. Pretty embarrassing, when you think about it.

'Don't just write me off as some Manic Pixie Dream Girl,' she said to me once. Well, that's exactly how I saw her. A Manic Pixie Dream Girl is a beautiful young woman with no desires of her own whose only real purpose is to distract the depressed male protagonist. To distract him, and to teach him a few important life lessons. Kate Winslet in *Eternal Sunshine of the Spotless Mind* is a good example of a Manic Pixie Dream Girl. Or Frida in *The History of My Sexuality* by Tobi Lakmaker.

As soon as Frida started going out with Arthur, I stopped sleeping in her bed. Arthur and Frida needed it to have sex, which is bullshit if you ask me – needing to lie in bed together so that you can have sex. They don't deserve any prizes for originality, those heterosexuals.

Since I couldn't sleep in Frida's bed any more, I alternated between the beds of her two best friends. When you can't sleep in a girl's bed any more for the simple reason that the girl in question is using it to have sex with her new lover, it's often time to take a hint. It's over, done – that's the hint you might want to take. I wasn't one to take a hint at that time in my life.

At that time in my life, I wasn't so smart. Then again, people in love usually *aren't*.

People in love are mostly preoccupied with the world, and even when they stop and think about it for more than three seconds, they conclude that the world's probably not going anywhere. Then they roll over and go back to sleep. They sleep really deeply, people in love do. Real morons – that's what they are. People in love are morons because they constantly forget that all those rosy colours they see aren't bursting from the world, they're just in their own moronic little heads. If you ask me, somebody should just tell them. They wouldn't believe it though – they're too moronic for that.

I think Lola and Lotti had a better sense of what was really going on. Lola and Lotti – those were the two friends that Frida lived with. Sometimes they gave me earplugs so I wouldn't have to listen to Frida's moaning. And in the morning, they'd make me a delicious breakfast while Frida and Arthur were still in bed. Come to think of it, I spent more time talking to Lola and Lotti than I did to Frida. They were reasonably nice. But after a while they got boyfriends too, and it became a real game of musical chairs in that house. You never knew which bed you could sleep in.

Believe it or not, Lola had a thing for that guy Dennis. And oddly enough, he just kept telling the same story. Some people only have one story. They tell it in the morning at breakfast, and by lunchtime they're telling it all over again. Lotti got involved with an older artist who had a lot of STDs. We were all a little afraid of him. On top of that, he was one of those artists whose day job consisted of telling other people that he was an artist. The rest of the time he was on his phone.

Or scratching himself. Can you imagine? On one side of the table is this guy going on about poop, and on the other side is an artist scratching himself. And as if that wasn't enough, Arthur would eventually wake up, and we'd all start planning our escape as soon as we heard him stumble out of bed. Arthur was one of those people who was absolutely certain that the whole world was waiting for him. It's really hard to put such an assumption into perspective, and we never fully succeeded.

When he came in, he started kissing everyone. Even Harry the Dirty Artist. Then he'd put on a record of the *Turkish Delight* soundtrack. Everything in the home of Lola, Frida and Lotti came from the seventies, when happiness was the norm. And happiness *was* the norm in that house. But I never managed to grab hold of it. Whenever that *Turkish Delight* song came on, they all thought of a red-haired girl hopping on the back of a bike. All I could think about was fast-spreading cancer.

Well, once Arthur had *his* music on, he could start making *his* breakfast. While he was doing that, everyone would make a break for it. The trick was to have left the living room by the time he turned round from the kitchen sink. It was almost as if he were counting to ten while we all ran off to hide. Lola usually fled to the university library, where she'd been working on a plan to write her thesis for years. Sometimes I wonder how many theses are actually written in the university library. I, for one, have never seen anyone doing anything productive there. At least, not *really*. Most people are just sitting around drinking coffee, preparing to start planning to actually do something – like write their thesis, for example. And you know what the funniest part about it is? Universities are supposed to *prepare* you for real life. But if all you want to do is run away from real life, I'd say go and hang out at the university library.

While Lola went to the library, Lotti usually went to the beach, which is pretty much the same thing as the library but with more fresh air. Harry the Dirty Artist usually went back to bed. And what Dennis did, nobody knew. Probably went off to work on his storytelling skills. Come to think of it, Dennis might have been the most productive of us all. In the end, I was the only one stupid enough to stay in my chair, which meant that, in the hours that followed, I was stuck there with Arthur and his unbridled happiness. Mostly, I just looked at Frida and tried to nod whenever she did. If you ever happen to run into Arthur, just nod and slowly retreat as quietly as possible. If you're lucky, he won't even notice you're gone.

Harry, oh Harry. Do you know what else he contracted? Scabies. Don't ask me how he got it. It's a question we asked ourselves hundreds of times, but after a while we gave up. Perhaps he had an affair with a woman from Classical Antiquity or a South American street dog. Anything was possible. Scabies are these little mites that live under your skin. They dig tunnels and reproduce. Can you imagine? There were *tunnels* under Harry's skin.

Well, people in love may be morons, but at least I was finally smart enough to get the hell out of that house. *Everybody* got it – Dennis, Frida, Lotti, of course – everybody. My mother had a conniption when she heard that I might have it too. She slapped me with a tea towel. Well, that certainly doesn't help against scabies. Worst-case scenario, your tea towel gets it too. I tried to tell her that, but she just kept shouting that I was 'disgusting'. And when someone is truly disgusted with you, they could slap you with a tea towel all day.

A few months later, I went with the scabies group to a film festival in Italy. All of the films were experimental, which is why I hardly left my tent the entire week. Not to sound rude, but I just don't *do* experimental films. I've also never really understood why people with a thirst for experimentation go into the arts. If you want to see things go wrong, you'd be better off working in a hospital.

Now, people from the experimental-film world would probably point out that sometimes things do go right, but sadly this isn't true. We've chosen the word 'experimental' very carefully and only use it to refer to failed experiments. Successful experiments are generally referred to as good films.

That week, Frida broke up with Arthur, which meant that Arthur spent the entire week crying in my tent. Between sobs, he shared all his insights about love. He said that love was a *garden*, and you had to decide for yourself where you wanted to harvest your flowers. Look, this is exactly the type of metaphor you don't want to bother me with for too long. I might nod patiently at first, but after a while I can't take it any more, and I snap. Then, things get *serious*.

So, here's what I did: I yawned for a while, a long while,

hoping he'd get the message. But Arthur wasn't one to pick up on signals. So I let him have it. I said that there was a world of broken hearts and a world of whole hearts. 'They are two beautiful worlds,' I said. 'Unfortunately, there's a third world too – the world of the heart that no one sees. The heart that people shit all over because it's a goddamn *lesbian* heart.'

Well, then I was on a roll. 'Nobody bothers to scrutinize *that* heart,' I shouted. When I'm really angry, I start using words like 'scrutinize'. 'Nobody bothers to scrutinize that heart, because all you people have only one hobby, and that is to *not* see us. No matter how friendly you are to us, you don't see us. Beat up the gays – great. But the lesbians? Stop right there! Who's going to beat us up?' I just kept screaming it, 'Who's going to beat us up? Where's our beating?' At that point, I started yelling in English for some reason, even though my English is really bad. 'Lesbians – do they even *exist*, when no one is watching?' Man, I was furious. Still am, actually.

Arthur started crying again, and because I'm cut from IKEA wood, I actually wanted to comfort him. But I couldn't because I tripped and fell to the ground. I'd been standing there in my sleeping bag the whole time. It was one of those ones with sleeves. So, there we were, Arthur still bawling his eyes out and me sprawled out on the ground in my sleeping bag. And that's how things ended with me and Frida – in a mess. It was like my mother once said: 'No matter what, love *always* ends in mayhem.'

There's No Novel in Here

For a long time, my publisher kept pestering me to write about the trip I made when I was eighteen. My publisher keeps pestering me about a lot of things, actually. They always want you to write a *novel*. Not very original if you ask me, which is why I stopped answering the phone when my editor called. After a while, she started calling me from a private number, but I still knew it was her. I'm telling you, people in the publishing industry really aren't the brightest.

You know what they kept saying about that trip I took when I was eighteen? 'There's a novel in here.' I hate to say it, but my publisher says that about pretty much everything. If you slip on a banana skin, she'll start calling. I might actually enjoy reading a book about someone who slipped on a banana skin. As far as I know, that almost never happens.

Since my publisher loves that phrase so much, I had an idea: I'd buy a bunch of little lockboxes, each one big enough to hold exactly one novel. Then I'd distribute them to all the publisher's employees, so they could exclaim, 'Why, there's a novel in here!' If the publisher ever needs an idea like that, she can always call me.

Anyway, the trip I took when I was eighteen was fairly remarkable. Originally, I wanted to cycle across Europe. That was why the Creep pinched my calves, remember? My plan was to write an amazing collection of poetry while cycling. Here's the most beautiful poem I wrote when I was eighteen:

> I would love to be tired
> of everything I've left undone
> and fall into a deep sleep
> not to lie awake worrying about it any more.

The poem was called 'Tired', and to be honest, I *was* pretty tired at the time. Eighteen-year-olds can get really tired. It's exhausting putting so much distance between who you're supposed to be and who you really are. Not the kind of exhaustion that I would feel sympathy for. They're cute little idiots, eighteen-year-olds. If you let them flutter around for long enough, they'll always come back, minus a few wings.

I won't bore you with the story for too long. But basically, my plan was to disappear. Actually, it all started with Bagels & Beans. I came up with the plan the week after I got fired because I was way too spacey. I didn't have the guts to tell my parents, so I just cycled around the city. It was the week I *disappeared*. Well, I wanted to disappear again – go away and come back only after I'd exceeded all expectations, you know?

So I bought a bike GPS and signed up for a weekend-long bicycle-repair workshop in Groningen. If I were you, I would never do a bicycle-repair workshop in Groningen. Nor would I do one in Brabant, or anywhere in the eastern part of the country. Actually, I wouldn't do one at all. No matter where you do it, you end up tinkering around with a bunch of halfwits. Sorry, but 'halfwits' is the only word to describe them. They hardly feed you anything, and all anyone wants to talk about are spokes.

But I did make one friend in the workshop. His name was Jack, and the great thing about him was that he didn't want to team up with anyone. They kept trying to make us change spokes and chains *as a group*. Well, Jack wasn't having it. On the first day, I sat down next to him, and he said, 'Hello there, little lady.' I liked that about him too, that he called me 'little lady'. At one point, he turned to me and said, 'I just dived in, little lady, and now I wonder if I'll ever come out again.' I asked him what exactly he dived into. 'The repair business,' he replied. Then he added, 'It's part of my personal grieving process.'

Now there's something that interests me – people with a personal grieving process. I stuck with him for the whole weekend. I just wanted to be around him, you know? Sometimes I had the urge to give him a pat on his hairy, crooked back, but then I remembered that his grieving process was personal. That's the thing about people in mourning: they can't see anyone else, only themselves. And maybe a few spokes.

One day before I left on my bike trip, it occurred to me: how on earth am I going to write a book of poetry if I'm pedalling the whole time? I was really brilliant like that when I was eighteen. So, at the last minute, I changed my plans.

Wild camping in the south of France: that's what I'd do. I'd camp in the wild and forage for my own food. Looking back, I think I'd watched *Into the Wild* a few too many times. Not a good idea. In *Into the Wild*, the main character forages for his own food. It all goes fine until he eats the wrong type of berry and dies. When you're stupid and eighteen, you think: just don't eat that berry. That's really the only lesson you take from the film.

At one point, the main character finds himself on this beautiful beach, and he has a revelation: 'And I also know how important it is in life not necessarily to *be* strong, but to *feel* strong. To measure yourself at least once.' So that's what I wanted to do: to measure myself at least once. And how did it go? Disastrously. I ended up at a deserted campground – it turns out that wild camping is illegal in the south of France.

In the south of France, it just *kept* raining. All day, pouring rain. Everything got soaked, and after a couple of days my air mattress was practically *floating* in my tent. It became a kind of raft, a raft on which I could lie down and think. I thought about how I'd lied to everyone, how I hadn't told anyone that I'd changed my plans. Everybody thought I was on my bike. It took me a whole month to send a message to the world that, upon reflection, I'd decided that my thighs weren't up to the challenge. But my thighs were fine, that wasn't the problem.

Sometimes you end up doing the weirdest things, when all you really want to do is disappear.

It was, in fact, my one and only attempt at genius, and that was as far as I got: me on an air mattress, floating around my one-person tent. And as if that wasn't bad enough, I ran into my most genius friend, Felix, in the south of France. Felix and I knew each other from high school, back when we had one hobby: correcting each other. The worst thing about it was that Felix was smarter than me, so he was actually the one doing the correcting.

With Felix, you could only think in hypotheses, and these hypotheses could either be confirmed or rejected. It drove me absolutely nuts. I just wanted to talk, you know, like I'm talking with you. But to Felix, all that mattered was being right. Later, I understood the relativity of being right, but not then. Back then, I just wanted to be right too.

Felix lived in Aix-en-Provence, where he was studying French and philosophy. His pronunciation was terrible, but his grammar was perfect, which got him a lot of curious looks from the French. I, on the other hand, had *excellent* pronunciation but hardly knew any words, so together we didn't get very far. After a while, we decided to meet up in the mountains, where we could be all alone with our hypotheses.

During one of our hikes, Felix started correcting me again, and each correction came with a very long explanation. Actually, you only had to spend three minutes in Felix's presence before he started explaining something to you. His explanations were usually impossible to follow, and on top of that, he was a really fast walker. The deeper he got into his explanation the faster he walked. So there I was, practically running after him, and that's when I started shouting at him.

Felix had become so engrossed in his own explanation that he'd walked into the middle of the road. So then we started arguing about that. We argued about whether it was better to keep left or right at a bend. With most people, an argument like that ends with a conclusion: left or right. But not with Felix – with him you just end up walking in the middle of the road because you've completely forgotten what you were talking about in the first place and what you're actually competing for is *space*.

Soon, that became our topic of conversation: the mind and its limits. You know what he said? He said I should read *The Catcher in the Rye*. He said that there was this one really *strong* passage – Felix's favourite passages were always *strong* – about the value of academic study. 'You'll learn to measure your mind and dress it accordingly.' Or something like that. Then he proceeded to talk about knowledge, and how some knowledge stays with you and other knowledge gets left behind, like a peel.

I really should read that book again. I started it, obviously. You know what the narrator says? He says: 'If you really want to hear about it, the first thing you'll probably want to know is where I was born, and what my lousy childhood was like, and how my parents were occupied and all before they had me, and all that David Copperfield kind of crap, but I don't feel like going into it, if you want to know the truth.' I thought that sentence was really strong, but also kind of sad. I felt sorry for David Copperfield, you know? I know it's only a novel, or a character from a novel, but you should still take characters into account.

That sentence made me want to call David Copperfield on the phone. I wanted to call him and say that I *was* interested in where he was born, and in his childhood and what his parents did before they had him. Come to think of it, I haven't told you any of those things about myself either.

Well, I was born at Slotervaart Hospital in Amsterdam-West after the midwife who showed up at the house turned out to be kind of strange and useless. My mother asked her if she was allowed to give birth at home in her own bed or if she had to go to the hospital. But the lady refused to answer the question. 'I can't answer that. That's not my job,' she said. Newsflash for all the midwives out there, that *is* your job.

Maybe this story isn't all that interesting. Maybe Salinger was right. I'm not going to tell you about my lousy childhood – we'd be here all night. What I will tell you is this: as a kid, I wanted to be Patrick Kluivert. Every hour of every day, I wanted to be the person who punted the ball into the net, winning the championship. Then I wanted to rip off my shirt and put it on again backwards. That's all I wanted.

But after a while, you just can't do it any more, because eventually the other kids in the playground will come up to you and say you have to keep your shirt on. They'll say you have to keep your shirt on because one day you're going to have breasts. But you don't even have breasts at that point, you know? There, that was my lousy childhood, and that's all I'm going to say about it.

So, here's what happens when you start arguing with Felix about whether you should walk on the left or the right side of the road. Before you know it, you're talking about somebody's *lousy* childhood. Oddly enough, right before those hikes with Felix, I'd signed up for the philosophy programme, and afterwards, I immediately withdrew. It was like with Patrick Kluivert, you know? He's the real thing, I thought, and I'm not.

Authenticity – a topic that *true* geniuses tend to overlook. Even Salinger overlooked it. I agree, by the way, about the peel. Some knowledge sticks with you and some doesn't – it's true. But still, something bothers me about it. Maybe it's because if people correct you often enough, whether about your shirt or some hypothesis you came up with, you start to lose your grip on which peel *really* belongs to you and which doesn't. It's already been decided for you, by *them*. You know what I mean?

After a while, I started getting tired of Felix and all his hypotheses, so I decided to hitchhike my way out of there. I ended up hitchhiking through Italy, which I really don't recommend. Nobody stops for you, I mean nobody, and finally after about three hours someone will come along and say: 'Never get into a car with Romanians,' and then drive off again. You know what's ironic? I hitchhiked halfway across Italy with Romanians. *Always* get into cars with Romanians, that's what I'd say. It's the Italians you have to worry about. I got into a car with an Italian one time, and within five minutes, he was feeling up my leg. I opened the door *while the car was still moving*, and basically rolled out with my backpack.

After that, I sat by the side of the road for several hours in the hot sun. When hitchhiking, it's better to stay on the main roads. But the guy had pulled off on to a small mountain road, so there I sat. And that's when I remembered – the bike GPS. I still had it with me. I didn't know what else to do, so I just typed in *Rome*. I was still pretty far north at that time, close to Pisa, but when you're sitting there with a half-empty water bottle staring down at the melting tarmac, you're bound to come up with some pretty strange ideas. On top of that, you shouldn't live in Amsterdam for too long. If you live in Amsterdam long enough, you assume that *everything* is about twenty minutes away.

Around nightfall, I was picked up by five Indian fishermen in a Mini Cooper. For those who have never been in a Mini Cooper, let me tell you – it's just big enough for four very thin people. And no fish. For the love of God, do not transport fish in a Mini Cooper, especially dead ones – *everyone* in the car will start smelling like them.

When we finally got to Rome, I didn't recognize anything from the last time I was there. Actually, the first time I was in Rome, I spent the whole time on a bus. Not one of those buses that take you past all the old buildings, but just – a parked bus. I was there on a school trip, and they wanted to send me home. But there wasn't any budget for it, so they just locked me in the bus. My parents didn't understand why all my pictures were taken from behind a window.

You want to know what happened? I got caught sneaking into other people's rooms at our hostel. Just for the fun of it. I wasn't up to anything, I swear. But eventually I ended up in Felicity's room. Felicity is an open book. As soon as I sat down on her bed, she beamed and started telling me how all the girls thought I was a fake girl. 'You sniff too much, and you swear all the time.'

When somebody says something like that to you, it makes you want to sniff even more and to shout all the curse words you can think of. But apparently, that's not an option any more. So I just wandered around the hostel feeling utterly miserable. I totally forgot that this wasn't allowed. I just looked at all the numbers on the doors, adding up how many girls thought I was fake. Then I lost count and started staring down at my fake-girl feet.

I was fully engrossed in the big toe on my right foot when Mrs Camel-Toe came storming down the hall. 'Oh for Christ's sake,' she snapped. 'That's it! I've had it with you.' She grabbed me by the collar and dragged me to her room. She pushed me down in a chair and went off to take a shower. And that's when I almost barfed. There, draped on the chair right in front of my face, was Mrs Camel-Toe's dirty underwear, and I know it's super-childish of me to tell you this, but there was a *ton* of discharge in the crotch.

It was bad. At first, it made me nauseous, but after a while I just felt sad again. When she walked out of the bathroom, she told me that this was my last warning. 'The next stop is

Schiphol Airport,' which honestly didn't sound so horrible to me. 'Just book me a fake seat on a fake aisle,' I thought.

The next day was a total disaster. I went for a drink with my fake friends on some fake square, but I still felt awful, so I left early. I called a taxi, but as soon as I got in the back, I realized that I didn't know the address of where we were staying. And the driver was *Italian*. Italians just don't speak English, like not a word. I'm pretty sure we drove around Rome for an hour.

In the end, he brought me back to the square he'd picked me up in because I knew how to walk back to the hostel from there. Naturally, the other girls had gone back by then, because proper girls are always on time.

Around three o'clock, I sauntered into the hostel and immediately ran into Mrs Camel-Toe. I could tell by the look on her face that she'd already been looking up flights on her phone. She seemed to be thoroughly enjoying herself. First, she made me write two hundred lines as punishment. I don't even remember what the sentence was. But it definitely wasn't anything about vaginal discharge or the address of the hostel. Such punishments rarely contain any useful information.

The next morning, I heard that there wasn't enough in the budget to put me on an early flight home, which is pretty funny in retrospect, but at the time I couldn't have cared less. They could've thrown me in prison for all I cared. When you're that sad, you're already locked up.

Well, those are my memories of my first trip to Rome. So you can imagine how great it felt to be free to explore the city. I wanted to take pictures of *literally* every building and send them to my parents. But I still couldn't shake the feeling that I needed to get out of there. Everywhere I went on that trip, I just thought, 'I need to get out of here.' That's the shitty thing about disappearing – it never really works.

It never works, and maybe that's why there's no novel in this story. You can race around the world searching for meaning and look for the words to capture that meaning. But you won't find anything, and you definitely won't find the words to capture it. There's really no point in travelling. You won't find anything – and definitely not yourself – you're always in way too much of a hurry for that. I spent the entire trip in a hurry, and all I found was despair. Despair because I thought that it would all just come to me if I could only put it into words. But nothing comes to you – even *if* you find the words to describe it.

Idiots, eighteen-year-olds, right? From Rome I took a bus to Prague. I watched *Crazy, Stupid, Love* four times in a row on that bus. I really like that movie. It probably drove the woman sitting next to me nuts. It's pretty hard to sleep with Ryan Gosling grinning in your face. But I actually like having Ryan Gosling grinning in my face. He says some pretty misogynistic things in that movie, and the movie itself really isn't that great, but sometimes you just have to watch it. You know what my favourite scene is? When Ryan Gosling takes off his shirt and Emma Stone says, 'Seriously? It's like you're *photoshopped.*' My problem is that I like to watch that scene *over and over again*. It's bad, I know, but for me it only gets funnier after the fourteenth time.

It turned out there was nothing to do in Prague. All there is to do is go to the Kafka Museum. I did that probably about fourteen times, too. The great thing about Kafka is that he was so unhappy. Not that this was evident in the museum, it's just something I read somewhere. And that's why the museum started to piss me off after a while. Everyone looked so damn cheerful, probably because they were about to have lunch. People in museums are mostly thinking about what they're going to do after they leave the museum. I just couldn't take it – not in *that* museum. Maybe it was because Franz Kafka made more or less the same mistake I did: he assumed that it would all come to him as long as he kept describing beautifully all the things he lacked. As far as I'm concerned, you shouldn't be thinking about your lunch in a place for a person like that.

When I wasn't in the Kafka Museum, I was in my room. I had rented it from two potheads in the suburbs. They were both women, and you know what the crazy thing about them was? They kissed each other. I really didn't know what to make of this at the time. It came to mind fairly often, but I just wasn't able to stick with the thought for too long.

I'm pretty sure the only poem I wrote on the whole trip was a love poem, to a breathtakingly beautiful woman I saw sitting on a terrace in Prague. I remember wanting to kiss her cheeks. That was all I wanted, to kiss her cheeks. I wondered about her lips, but I just couldn't imagine kissing them. I had the feeling that something *terrible* would happen if I even went near her lips.

After Prague, I went to Kraków, where the main tourist attraction is Auschwitz. It's advertised everywhere. In Amsterdam, we've got the Red Light District; in Kraków, they've got a concentration camp. It's weird, but true. I've always been pretty sensitive to advertising, so after a few days I signed up for a tour.

Ironically, you can only visit Auschwitz in *groups*, and since I was on my own they let me tag along with a school class. It was really odd, experiencing Auschwitz with a group of Polish schoolchildren. They were all on their phones, taking selfies at the gate and whatnot. In moments like that, you're almost sorry that there isn't one last Nazi walking around to teach people some discipline. By the time we got to Birkenau, the kids were all tired and hanging on each other. One boy even tried to lean on me; that's when I decided I'd had enough.

I just took off running, right there in Birkenau. I just kept running until those kids were out of sight. The only problem was that I didn't pay any attention to where I was going and lost my bearings. Maybe you didn't know this, but Auschwitz-Birkenau is this massive open space, and I felt like I had to walk every inch of it. It was important that my feet touched every inch of ground because I wanted to make sure my ancestors would *feel* me. Really silly, I know, but I had to do it. My neck got sunburnt after a while because I kept bending forward to make sure I didn't miss a spot. Sometimes I'm such an idiot. But then again, I don't know how you could *not* be an idiot in a place like that.

When I really had no idea where I was any more, I put in my iPod earbuds and listened to Bob Dylan. You know what song I put on? 'Blowin' in the Wind'. It just seemed appropriate. But as soon as I realized that Bob Dylan didn't have anything useful to say about it either, I yanked them out. People always act like Bob Dylan has an answer for everything, but he really doesn't. Bob Dylan is just one limited man. And he's looking more and more like a tortoise these days. Which has nothing to do with it, of course, but it's true.

While I was studying the wrinkles on Bob Dylan's face, a woman pulled on my arm. She snarled something at me in Polish and motioned for me to move along. She was barely five feet tall, which was good because it meant I could keep one eye on the ground.

We crossed half of Birkenau together, until we arrived at the entrance, and she plopped down on a chair next to the bathrooms. It turned out that she was the Auschwitz bathroom attendant. Can you imagine? I think about her a lot, almost every day in fact. Then I wonder if everyone actually paid the entrance fee, and if there weren't some Polish schoolchildren who tried to sneak in. A terrible thought, but I'm sure it happens. Some things happen everywhere.

Before I boarded the train out of that deranged city, there was this guy who tried to kiss me. I haven't told you about any of that yet, but there were a lot of men who tried to kiss me on that trip. It was nuts. And you know, it was funny. *When you're a girl* travelling alone, nobody asks you if you want to be a poet, or what your favourite story by Kafka is. *Nobody* would ask you questions like that. Actually, if you want to hear about all the men who didn't ask me questions like that, I might as well start this story over from the beginning.

Anyway, it was always the same. I'd fall asleep on the train, and when I woke up, everyone in the compartment would be staring at me. Actually, I don't really like to talk about it. Either they're staring at you or they're trying to talk to you or if you're really lucky, they might even be jerking off to you. And of course, each sounds worse than the last, but it's all the same really. It all boils down to the same thing; it just takes a little while to figure that out.

After a while, you don't even care any more. You wake up in one of those compartments, and the only thought running through your mind is that you need to find your book of Kafka's short stories. Why? Because Kafka doesn't look back. The guy could tell a hell of a story, but what I liked most about him was this: he never looked back.

When you travel *as a girl*, you don't learn anything about the world. All you learn is that there's a way of looking at the world that doesn't belong to you. And it's funny because I already know that some of you will think I'm exaggerating here. I wish I were, but I'm not. At every hostel I stayed in I made sure to get the top bunk just so I could keep a lookout. On every train, I sat next to the aisle so I could make a quick getaway. And on every street, I kept my eyes locked on the damn paving stones just to make sure I didn't send the wrong *signal*. Those paving stones were more or less the same as the ones we have in Amsterdam. I didn't travel all that way to look at stupid paving stones. But that's what you learn *as a girl* travelling alone.

Well, the guy who tried to kiss me at the station in Kraków wasn't the worst of them. Every morning at the hostel, I woke up to find him standing next to my bed waiting to ask what I was doing that day. 'Going to Auschwitz,' I replied, but that didn't deter him. You know what he said? He said he wanted to come and visit me in Amsterdam. That's another thing – the guys were always saying that they were going to come and visit me in Amsterdam. If they actually had come, the city would have needed a special hostel to house them all.

The last stop on my trip was Sweden, where wild camping *is* allowed, so I could finally forage for my own food and be receptive to poetry. Little tip for people who want to be receptive to poetry – don't go wild camping. Actually, just don't go wild camping at all. Especially not in Sweden. You know why? Because in Sweden a loaf of bread costs like ten euros. So, if you're dumb enough, you'll end up buying nothing but yogurt and cottage cheese because they're a tiny bit more affordable.

The problem with yogurt and cottage cheese is that you have to keep them cold, which is impossible while wild camping. Therefore, you spend much of your day worrying about your dairy products going sour. The rest of the time you're worrying about being murdered. Fortunately, it doesn't get dark in Sweden in the summer, so you can spend the whole night sitting outside your tent, fiddling with yogurt and cottage cheese and thinking about your mortal remains.

After about seventy-two hours (when it doesn't get dark you start thinking in hours rather than days), I walked back to the local train station. I don't think I'd ever longed for Amsterdam as much as I did that night. After a while, you just start to miss everything. You miss the traffic crossings where no one knows who has right of way, so everybody just starts cursing each other. You miss the benches along the canal where everybody throws their rubbish on the ground, and you have no idea whether it will ever be picked up. Eventually, you even start to miss the congestion of the *Kennedylaan*, you know?

Well, the stupid thing was that I couldn't just go home. I wanted to, but I hadn't been away for very long. Only a couple of months, and my plan was to be gone for at least half a year. So – and I know this sounds ridiculous – I decided to stay at the train station. It was completely deserted, day and night. The only person around was Gustav, the cleaner. Of all the men I met, he might be the only one I wouldn't have minded visiting me in Amsterdam someday. He'd bring me croissants and a cup of coffee. Then he'd be on his way, and I could lie down and relax. Swedish train stations have floor heating, so they're really nice to lie on.

I also stopped worrying about being murdered. The world becomes very manageable in a small-town train station. You know exactly when the train is coming, and you don't need to worry about catching it because you weren't planning to anyway. Other than that, you just look forward to seeing Gustav. He and I didn't talk much, just a few words. That's the best – when someone just gives you a cup of coffee and leaves you alone. He might *wonder* whether you're a poet or what your favourite Kafka story is – but he just hands you the coffee and goes. It's really the best. And after a while, you start to forget that you're a poet yourself and stop thinking about all the things you've left undone.

Yellow Tuesdays

As calming as a small-town train station might be, after a few days you've had your fill of croissants and floor heating. In the end, I got on a train and started making my return journey to Amsterdam. When I got back, I sat down on one of those benches along the canal covered in rubbish that you're not sure anyone will ever pick up. I hadn't slept in a long time. When you haven't slept for a really long time, you're bound to do something weird. Suddenly, you have these *ideas*. I came up with the idea of lying down on one of those benches and just waiting for somebody to come and get me. I hoped that somebody would just start calling out my name. Like when your parents call you for dinner.

When your parents call you for dinner, you generally stall for a minute. You never rush to the table. That's what I wanted. I wanted someone to come and get me so I could stall for a minute. But I was so incredibly tired that I started to doze off.

I was half asleep when I felt somebody jab me in the stomach with a truncheon. It wasn't a jab really, more of a poke. And the guy wasn't a real cop, he was just one of those neighbourhood watch people. 'What is it that you people do, exactly?' I wanted to ask. I've never understood what the neighbourhood watch actually does. But this guy didn't seem particularly interested in discussing such matters.

He told me that there were plenty of hotels on the Lijnbaansgracht. 'And shelters,' he added. And that's when I felt the tears well up in my eyes. I just started raging at the guy, you know? I raged that there was so much rubbish to clean up around the bench and I could keep sitting there if I wanted. Then I raged that there was nobody who loved this city as much as I did and that my mother's side of the family had lived in Amsterdam for generations. Then I started going on about how many times they had to move and how terrible the living conditions were back then. All of a sudden, I was *furious* about it. I told him that the Lakmakers' financial situation only improved when my grandfather went to medical school, and that he was one hell of a doctor until he decided to hang himself because Auschwitz comes for *everyone* in the end. Can you believe that? I told the neighbourhood watch guy that Auschwitz comes for *everyone* in the end.

Well, I still don't quite understand what the neighbourhood watch does, but I now know that they're not interested in conversations about death camps in Poland or the history of housing in Amsterdam. You know what he did? He started poking me again with his club and pushing me back. 'Hey now, woah!' I roared. When I don't know what to say next, that's what I shout. 'Hey now, woah!' I yelled over and over again and then I almost fell into the canal because it was dark, and we could hardly see a thing. The Lijnbaansgracht is generally poorly lit, with lots of rubbish around the benches.

After that, I went over to Fenna's. The last thing I wanted to do was go home to my parents. I sat on her stoop for a while, and when it was finally a more *Christian* hour, I rang the doorbell. Fenna wasn't home. But her dad was, and he invited me in for coffee. You know what the great thing about Fenna's dad is? He gets those sharp pains in his chest when he gets anxious too. He told me that once. After somebody shares something like that with you, you're safe with them for the rest of your life. So I just started telling him everything, from Aix-en-Provence to Sweden.

I told him that I wanted to be a Russian translator and that one day I might be entrusted with the works of Chekhov and Turgenev. That was another idea I came up with on the spot. I beamed as I told him. I hardly touched the coffee. Suddenly, I wanted to tell him everything.

Fenna's dad was quiet for a long time, and then you know what he said? He said that I had a *lively, intense* mind, and whatever I did, it would all be fine. Believe it or not, I started crying again. But in a completely different way than I did with that neighbourhood watch guy. I cried like I would later cry with Czarina – passionately, for everything. For everything, and mostly because it was going to be fine. And I cried for *him* too. Because he knew what those sharp pains felt like, and he was still here. It's hard to explain, but at that time in my life I really wasn't so sure about it myself – how long I would still *be* here.

I told you that I suddenly wanted to tell him *everything*, didn't I? That's what I did. I had known Fenna since high school, and through my tears I told him that she was the only person I'd ever felt truly comfortable with, because Fenna was just Fenna – and nothing else. And I wasn't just saying that to *please* him, by the way. I really meant it. I said that I'd been wrong about everything, wrong about the guys, wrong about the girls, and then I started telling him about all that too, about the guys and the girls.

First I told him about the girls, about how I always felt like I wasn't one of them, especially at school dances, which were absolutely horrible. Whenever there was a school dance, the four of us – Fenna, Betsie, Zahra and me – would go together. Zahra always got asked to help out at the school's open day because somewhere way back in her family's history she had 'multicultural' ancestors, and St Ignatius School wanted to present itself as being open to everybody. But St Ignatius School was anything but open to everybody. In reality it was a school for one type of student – the Philip de Koning type.

Philip de Koning was one of those guys who always said, '*Rrrright*, but . . .' – you know what I mean? Philip de Koning was unbelievable. In our first year of high school, he spent a long time trying to convince me that it wasn't enough to hang out with people from Amsterdam-Zuid – they also had to be from the *right part* of Amsterdam-Zuid. Can you imagine? The right *part* of Zuid. The neighbourhood behind the Olympiaplein was technically Zuid, but it was for *renters*. Unbelievable, I'm telling you.

Getting ready for the school dance was rough, mainly because Fenna and I were significantly uglier than Betsie and Zahra. It was like a contest, only the winners had been decided in advance. It was mostly between Betsie and Zahra, and in the hours leading up to the dance, they pushed each other to the limit. They were both really good at doing make-up. Fenna and I were not.

It usually started with eye make-up. Fenna would poke herself in the eye with the mascara three times and decide she'd had enough. Then she'd go off and check the football scores. But I didn't know where to stop. I did everything Zahra and Betsie did, but with terrifying and far-reaching consequences.

Zahra and Betsie were usually going for *smoky* eyes, which involves eyeliner above your eyelashes and dark eye shadow. It looked really good on them. And that was the problem – there I was trying to put on eyeliner, and all I could do was stare at how beautiful they were. On top of that, you need a steady hand to put on eyeliner, and my hand is not steady at all. My hand shakes. In the end, I had smoky eyes too, but in a more literal sense – as if my eyes had been smoked out.

Zahra would see me in the mirror and shriek, 'Sof, you look like a panda again!' I always looked like a panda. Then Zahra and Betsie started applying foundation. A tip for anyone – be they person or panda – who wants to apply foundation: choose the right shade. When it comes to foundation, it's all about finding the right shade. It should be selected with the utmost care at Douglas, where you'll be helped by employees who have dutifully smeared on every shade of foundation ever made. It would take an *archaeologist* to excavate down to their original faces, which is why I wouldn't trust them.

Then there was the fact that one time I went to Douglas with Felicity, and she stole a whole bunch of stuff. Word to the wise: if you're planning on shoplifting, don't invite me to come. Trust me. I'll start by being obnoxiously friendly with all the employees and shake hands with everyone on the way out. To make up for it, you know? And the whole time, I won't blink. I'll just stare at all the products with my eyes wide open and pace the floor at high speed. I'll literally race up and down the aisles, as if I were planning to buy *everything*.

Well, Felicity and I got caught, of course. We didn't have to go to the police station, but incidents like that can really damage your relationship with a business. I didn't go to that shop any more, and I didn't have any foundation of my own. So in the end, I just used Zahra's, but given that she was mixed race, her skin was a few shades darker than mine. Also, when applying foundation, it's important to rub it in really well so it blends with your skin tone. I always forgot to do that, which is why I usually went to school dances looking like a panda with an oddly brown head attached to a pale white neck.

The sweet thing about Fenna was that she never said a word about it. She didn't mind if I sat down next to her with my inky black eyes and weirdly brown cheeks. I must've looked like some kind of scarecrow, but she never said anything. She'd just start talking about FC Barcelona's defence, and how the prevailing opinion was that the left back needed replacing. I loved those moments. They were the only moments when I felt like I could breathe a little, you know?

Then the drinking started. Betsie and Zahra spent at least an hour in the bathroom doing God knows what. I hate to say it, but *women. My god.* They already look perfect, but they still have to spend an hour in the bathroom. That hour is precisely what separates me from women. And you know what's funny? If you try to tell women that they already looked perfect an hour ago, they'll get mad. You're supposed to say that they look perfect *now*. As if that one hour was absolutely critical.

But for me and Fenna that hour *was* critical. We needed to drink so that we could forget how much prettier Zahra and Betsie were and how all the boys were about to begin grinding on us. That's what the school dances were all about – having some sweaty teenage boy rub his erection against your leg.

The four of us would always dance in a circle, anxiously waiting to see who would be groped first. Of course, I just went along with it. That was the awful thing about high school, you had to participate. Everybody did, except Zahra. Whenever some guy tried to grind against her from behind, she'd step forward and ask him what the *hell* he was doing. Nobody had successfully grinded on Zahra since our first year. The only thing the guys did do was ask me when Zahra was going to loosen up. All I could do was shrug – if anyone wanted to grind on Zahra it was me, but those times just weren't made for that.

So, I started telling all this to Fenna's dad. And I could tell that it made him wonder about everything, you know? I loved that – adults who nodded, just wondering. So I went on. I told him about the guys, and why I was wrong about them too.

The guys, my god. They fascinated me. In my first year of high school, I made a really good friend, Chiel. He was Arnon, and I was Rosie. Arnon and Rosie are the two main characters in the book *Blue Mondays* by Arnon Grunberg who mostly just walk down the Apollolaan talking about sex. That's what Chiel and I did too – we walked down the Apollolaan and fumbled about a bit with each other's genitals. That's the nice thing about being thirteen: you don't really have to do anything with your genitals yet. You can just have a bit of a fumble and go home.

Chiel had already had his growth spurt in eighth grade, so everyone called him the Paedo when we kissed. Chiel and I kissed all over the place: by the bike rack, by the lockers, under the Hilton Hotel. We always hoped that the Ajax team would be staying there, and that they'd start heckling us. That never happened, but one time Dennis Bergkamp walked by and didn't say a word.

Every morning, Chiel doused himself in Lynx deodorant. I think he'd seen one of those commercials where the guy sprays a little in the air and women start attacking him from all directions. But the girls weren't exactly jumping all over Chiel – it was just me, which is why I always smelled faintly of Lynx. I pretty much lived in Chiel's armpit, or more precisely, in the armpit of the Mahler T-shirt that he always wore. Maybe that's why I let him feel my crotch so often: deep down, I knew that his true loyalty was to Mahler and Mahler alone.

Chiel's main ambition was to become a horn player, and he succeeded. The realization that he was going to succeed finally sank in a year before we graduated, and that's when things started to change between us. You really shouldn't get too close to people who want to achieve something and then actually succeed in achieving it. It changes them. They don't see *you* any more.

The funny thing is that it doesn't really make them any happier. They just become more independent, and a little cocky. And man, did Chiel get cocky. We stopped kissing around that time. We just talked, and all that talking slowly became hell. He became good friends with Felix – you know, the smart one. And it's weird, but as soon as Felix came into the picture, Chiel didn't laugh at my jokes any more.

I should mention that whenever you're in the company of two guys who consider themselves *promising*, don't expect them to laugh at your jokes. Promising young men are incredibly exhausting. What exactly they promise, no one knows, but they will spend the entire lunch break making sure that you know just how promising they are. We'd talk about Mahler, or Ajax, and whatever I tried to say came out wrong. I think it was because they never made eye contact with me – that's one way to recognize the promising types: they only make eye contact with you once they've made their point. And they always have a point to make, believe me.

Eventually, it got so bad that Chiel started patting me on

the shoulder whenever I tried to tell a joke. 'That was cute,' he'd say. Well, I don't know if you've ever tried to tell a joke, but that is generally not the reaction you're going for. Then he'd start going on about the stand-up comedian Micha Wertheim, and how his last show was so *strong*, even though I already knew that because we went to the show together. And it sounds crazy, but after a while you start thinking you no longer exist. You start hearing the opening line of Nescio's *Amsterdam Stories* in your head: 'We were titans – but good titans?' And then you realize that's not even what the line says. It's 'We were boys – but good boys. If I may say so myself.'

That's really the worst thing about hanging out with promising boys: you constantly catch yourself making mistakes. Until you take a good, hard look at that opening sentence. When you really look at it, you realize it's all pointless. You realize that everything's already been written, and you will never be able to make a point – let alone be right.

Fenna's dad *applauded* when I said this. I'm so tired of men applauding after I've just ripped their species to shreds. As if what I've just said is for *them*. I'm just saying it for myself, you know? But he wanted me to go on about Felix and Chiel, so I did for a little while.

I told him how things ended between me and those *promising* boys. It was on a beach in Mallorca. We were there on our graduation trip, and while everyone was making out at the club, we were sitting by the shore, exchanging hypotheses. Chiel's hypothesis was 'integrity is the only thing that counts'.

Felix and I nodded. Then he looked out across the water and said, 'Guys, I think we're *category Grunberg.*'

What I wanted to say was, 'No, you were Arnon, and I was Rosie, and now we're nothing but a bunch of stupid dreams.' But oddly enough, Chiel and Felix really seemed to believe those dreams. That one day it would all be ours. They really believed it. I vividly remember this hope, and especially how I struggled to cherish it the same way they did. The only thing I dared to hope was that I really saw them – more clearly than they saw me. And that one day that look would give *me* the words.

'Bravo!' cried Fenna's dad at last. And that's what hurt – you dare to share your sorrows, and once again it's taken for entertainment. Which is why, in the end, I still went home to my own house. A few years later, I wrote my first short story about Felix and Chiel. It was called 'Young Titans', and I won't bother you with it because it's more or less the same story I've just told you.

But I did perform it, not that long ago actually, on 24 April 2019, if I'm not mistaken. Of course, I'm not mistaken. It was the day after my mother died, and those are the kinds of days you don't forget. Afterwards, I stood outside in the pouring rain, and a woman came up to me and said, 'How terrible it must be to have so much talent.'

It is, actually. And you know what she said then? 'It kind of reminded me of Grunberg's *Blue Mondays.*' It's a comparison that I've heard as many times as Sallie Harmsen forgot my name. I can just feel it coming. But that night, I didn't care any more.

I lit a menthol cigarette, which is something I do when I'm really sad, exhaled the nauseating smoke and sighed. 'You know, maybe I should just call it "Yellow Tuesdays".'

Quite a few people had gathered around us by then, and they all laughed. It was so weird, you know? When you've just picked out the sweater your mum will wear, because *nobody* else dares to do it because they all know she's never going to wear *another* sweater; when you've just picked out the sweater that your mother will wear in her *coffin* which is made of oak even though you've never thought about oak in your life; well, you just don't expect the people around you to ever laugh again. But they do laugh, even though it's raining really hard and the air reeks of menthol cigarettes. They laugh, while all you can think about is oak, but not really, because when you think about oak, no image comes to mind.

III

ELIAS
WELVERLOREN

Elias Welverloren

Believe it or not, my mother was extremely sick throughout this *entire* story. It was kind of like that artificial mosquito buzzing sound, you know which one I'm talking about? It's been gone for a while now, but it was this sharp, high-pitched sound that only young people could hear, and they used it to clear hangout spots. That's the crazy thing about someone who's extremely sick, and sometimes only a little sick. When someone is extremely sick and sometimes only a little sick, it's constantly buzzing in the background. It's always there, but there's not much to say about it.

Fifteen minutes after my mother told me she was terminally ill, I had to go to work. I was working for Foodora at the time, which is gone now too. It was this delivery company that basically offered the same service as Deliveroo. That's probably why they went out of business: they offered the same service as Deliveroo. That afternoon on my bike, all I could think about was what I would wear to the funeral. I'd never worn a suit before, you know? I just kept thinking about what kind of fabric I'd choose, and that I'd have to have it tailored to fit my narrow shoulders.

It's stupid really, you hear news like that and all you can think about is how narrow your shoulders are, and whether the tailors at Oger will know what to do with them. But I didn't go to Oger when my mother died. I just wasn't in the mood. I already knew how it would go. They'd look at me like I was a fifteen-year-old boy, or a woman. And at Oger, they don't lift a finger for women or fifteen-year-old boys. They would try to send me somewhere else, and if that happened, I was afraid I might explode. After losing your mother, the tiniest things can set you off.

My dad did end up going to Oger, and not that it's relevant, but he found himself standing next to King Willem-Alexander. It was a few days before King's Day, so Willem-Alexander was making the rounds. Can you imagine? There you are trying on black suits for your wife's funeral, and you have to step aside because *the King* just stumbled in. Now that would have definitely set me off.

When we found out my mother was terminal, it was the third time she'd had cancer. My mother spent a ridiculous amount of her life with cancer. The first time she was diagnosed, I was eighteen and on my way out to meet Douchebag D. I remember it well. I was just about to hop into the shower when she called me into her study. She mumbled that they'd found something in her intestines. I nodded and said that I was about to take a shower – I was standing there in my underwear, you know? I was literally *stepping into* the shower. Just before I left the room, I asked, 'So it's cancer?' And she said yes. But she'd already turned back to her computer so I couldn't see her face. Sometimes these things can unfold in the strangest ways. You expect there to be an orchestra playing or something, but there just isn't.

After I'd showered, I called Chiel. He said he already had a feeling that I was going to call him with bad news. It's funny – even when you call to say that your mother is terminally ill, the promising young men of the world will still jump at the opportunity to show off how erudite they are. Then I called Fenna, who said, 'Well, now you're one of those people whose mum has cancer.' Obviously, there was no arguing with that. Then I called Betsie, and she said she really needed to catch the bus. Finally, I called Zahra, and at least she didn't say anything. She just started to cry.

Then I played Hot Dog Bush for a long time. Hot Dog Bush is this computer game where you're George W. Bush and you have to run a hot dog stand. You start out in a New York City slum, and at first it's just hot dogs. But the longer you play, the harder it gets. Eventually, you have to sell fries too, and once you get to Manhattan, then come the onions. Those onions made me a nervous wreck. They just burned so fast, you know?

My mother had surgery at Slotervaart Hospital. Her doctor was Jewish, and so we all thought she was in safe hands. But that hospital was a mess. They forgot to schedule her follow-up appointments and we forgot to call, because that's all you want to do after an ordeal like that: forget, forget, forget.

Three years later, she fell down the stairs in the middle of the night. She was wearing my father's slippers, which were about five sizes too big, and she tripped. Staircases in Amsterdam's Oud-Zuid are really long, by the way. She broke her neck, and the fire department had to come and get her. I wasn't there, because again, I was lying next to Frida. Or in a room next to Frida's, where she and Arthur were lying. I don't remember exactly. All I remember is that I had eight missed calls from my dad, and when I finally called back he said that things didn't look so bad. That's another strange thing – when something truly awful happens, people always try to assure you that it's really not so bad.

She was taken to the VU Medical Center, where they diagnosed her with multiple forms of cancer. They saw it on the scans. They weren't even looking for cancer, but they found it, you know? I didn't call anyone then. Not even Zahra. I just sat there playing Hot Dog Bush. The first thing I thought about were the onions, how I couldn't let them burn.

The VU Medical Center turned out to be a mess too. First they botched the operation and left a piece of plastic sticking out of her neck. Then it turned out that they'd misinterpreted the scans and she really only had cancer in one place: her liver, which meant she had to go under the knife again. The day after the surgery, I ran into Rose at SC Buitenveldert, and she held me for a long time because, naturally, I was crying again. 'Dushi, it's gonna be okay,' she said. 'Even if it's not.' Those kinds of statements are really frowned upon in philosophy. But sometimes philosophy isn't very helpful. Sometimes you just need to hear that it's going to be okay even if it's not, and you don't give a damn what Wittgenstein would have to say about it.

A year later, it was back. That was the first thing they said. The second thing was that it wasn't going to go away, not ever. Well, they didn't say it like that. What they said was: 'All we can offer you at this point is palliative care.' I swear, if you need someone to beat around the bush for you, just call the VU Medical Center. Everybody there is dying, but they'd rather throw themselves off the roof than look you in the eye and tell you the truth.

From that moment on, we knew, and we never talked about it again. I did write a poem about it once, but I never finished it. It began like this: 'My mother, my greatest void, though still we eat here now.' But maybe that *was* the whole poem. It's quite something to watch someone die. All you can think is, 'though still we eat here now'. You see the void, but it's not there. You feel the absence, but it's not there – or not yet at least, which is why nobody talks about it.

Nobody except Kyra, of course, who took me in her arms and cried, saying, 'These are *your* tears, Lakkie, *your* tears!' I think that's why I loved Kyra so much – because she showed me how to live. But we didn't live, we just watched closely as everything slowly became less: the coffee dates, the nights out, the birthday parties. My mother died very slowly. And you know what the worst thing is? That you have to go through something like that alone. I really don't have a lot of wisdom to share with you, but this I know: that's the worst thing about it. It's not the dying – death doesn't exist, there's only life. It's the loneliness, that's the worst thing. It always has been, and it always will be.

Actually, that's what I've been trying to tell you this whole time. That loneliness is the worst thing there is, and I want you to know what it looks like – from the outside. After that, I swear I'll leave you alone. We can all go our separate ways, as cold as that sounds.

The night before my mother died I was wearing a T-shirt and matching red-and-white Adidas trainers. I'm a loser like that sometimes. I like my clothes to match. Stupid, I know. I'd spent the afternoon re-reading *The Trial* by Kafka, and you know what struck me? That the guy was really funny. People are always trying to overcomplicate Kafka, but if you ask me, they just don't understand him. He was just this guy with no talent for punchlines trying to crack a joke. So people ended up taking his work so seriously when all he ever wanted to do was make them laugh.

It was a really hot night. I called up my mother to tell her how everyone had misunderstood Kafka. 'Is that so, my sweet girl?' she said. It's lovely really, my mum always called me 'my sweet girl'. At such moments, you *really* don't feel like explaining that you might feel different, and that the word 'girl' doesn't quite fit. It's strange, but when someone is so sick that all she can do is drink tea, and only if the bag has been dipped in and out very quickly because otherwise it's too strong, those things don't matter any more. You start speaking your own kind of language, and oddly enough, no one else seems to understand it. You talk about all kinds of stuff, from Ajax to Kafka, but you're actually *saying* something else. Do you get what I'm saying? It's okay if you don't.

But here's the crazy thing: she fell asleep. I was just talking to her, not about Kafka any more, but something else, and she fell asleep. She didn't hang up; she just stopped talking. I was standing there in the middle of the Leidseplein and everyone started honking at me – the trams, the cars; even people on their bikes started ringing their bells – and don't ask me why, but suddenly it hit me: this is it. This is life. All the honking and ringing because nobody ever knows who has right of way and everybody always has somewhere to be. Actually, I wanted to stand there forever, you know? Amsterdam traffic is no stranger to weird behaviour, I thought – people will learn to live with me.

There were a whole bunch of people in the kitchen, my dad and my brother of course, but also Djoeke, my mum's best friend, and her boyfriend. Well, believe it or not, *he* was the one who told me that things were going downhill. That kind of thing really bothers me. I'll decide if my mother is dying, thank you very much. So I stayed in the kitchen for a long time, without going upstairs. Then someone said there was a hole in my Ajax shirt, and that's when I snapped. Some people just don't understand when it's okay to comment on someone else's fanwear. It's just a nice jersey, you know? Not one of those new ones, but an old one, with a collar.

My mother had been sleeping in my old room because it was at the back of the house, and it was the only place where you didn't hear the Hummers rumbling by all day long. In Oud-Zuid, all you hear are Hummers thundering down the street. When I finally went in, she was asleep with her iPod next to her. She was listening to *The Diary of Anne Frank*. Endearing, really. The diary was read by Carice van Houten. 'Carice reads too fast,' was my mother's initial reaction. 'Carice does a terrific job,' she said later. It's funny, it wasn't like my mum actually knew Carice van Houten. But she still called her Carice, as if she were reading aloud to her in that room, you know?

I still have that iPod. Sometimes I listen to it on shuffle, and suddenly I hear Carice van Houten's voice: 'June 1942.' It always scares the shit out of me. Who wants to go back to June 1942? June 1942 was a time when everything was about to go wrong, but hadn't gone wrong yet – for Anne Frank, I mean. As for me, I've had enough of that for a lifetime – things being *just about* to go wrong, but not quite.

'It's a lost cause, my sweet girl,' my mum said to me when she woke up. 'Boats against the current,' I replied. She had no idea what I meant by that, and neither did I. That's the worst thing about it: in moments like that, you want so badly to say the right thing that you start mumbling something stupid. And then she fell back to sleep.

That evening I was going to cook for my dad and brother, but I just couldn't bring myself to go to Albert Heijn. You can't just walk into a plain old grocery store when your mother is dying. So I went to Organic instead. That's this store that you'd only ever shop at if your mother were dying. It's for people who need tangible proof that nothing makes sense and who are therefore willing to pay seven euros for a bag of pasta. I think I paid about thirty euros for a handful of products, and you know what I felt like saying? I felt like saying, 'Make it sixty.' The hell with it, you know?

And it was the weirdest thing, but that night, the temperature just didn't cool down. Not after my mum laid her hand on my neck while I hovered over her and promised that I would *always* come back. Not after I saw my father cry, and he mumbled that there would be a lot more tears in the days to come. Not when my brother told me that he was leaving to watch *Game of Thrones*, or when the family doctor came by to say that she could, *technically speaking*, die that night. The temperature just didn't cool down.

And it's funny, people always ask *when* my mother died. 'A few minutes ago,' is what I want to say, because that's how it is, you know? That's really what I want to say when people ask me that – I want to hold up my right arm, look down at my watch and say, 'A couple of minutes ago.' And undoubtedly there'll be someone who'll try to tell me that a watch belongs on your left wrist, to which I will reply that *nothing* belongs, *nothing* makes sense, not even my watch, which has been frozen on a few minutes after half past eight for an awfully long time now.

Because that's the answer to their question: she died at half past eight in the morning, while my dad was in the shower. I'd like to do it too someday – leave when no one is looking.

She died at half past eight, and my dad called twice to tell me, but I didn't answer because I was still sleeping. When I called him back, he said that my mother had passed away and that he was going to make coffee.

After I hung up the phone I took a long shower, an extremely long shower, and hit my left hand against the wall to my right in the hope that somebody might see. But there was nobody there, nobody at all, and all it did was hurt my left hand.

When I walked into the house, the doctor was standing in the hall and said, 'Shall we go in together?' But we didn't go in together, I went in alone, and when I walked into the room I fell to my knees. I just crouched there on my knees and held my head in my hands. And suddenly I knew exactly what to say. I didn't want to say something like 'boats against the current'; I wanted to say a hundred other things, and I did.

You know what I said? I said that I would manage. And a hundred other things, of course, but that's mostly what I said: that I'd be fine. And it's so stupid, you know? Because I said it too late, and now she'd never know for sure. That was the terrible thing: *I* knew, all of a sudden I knew for sure. I knew that I had a lively, intense mind, but that no matter what I did, it would be okay. I knew that I would feel those sharp pains in my chest a million more times, but that didn't mean they were always right. But I said it too late.

She was just lying there, and she was so incredibly cold. I found it almost excessive, how cold she was. I get it, she's dead, I thought. It looked so strange – to see her lying there in my old room with the walls covered in Manchester United posters. I liked Ajax back then too, but I was even more into Manchester United. Edwin van der Sar was their goalie at the time, and that man just radiates *calm*. So, there she was, just lying there, surrounded by posters of Van der Sar in his yellow jersey. It was actually kind of ridiculous when you thought about it.

I used to be afraid of cold bodies, but I wasn't any more. I leaned in very close and kissed her. Her lips felt dry, way too dry, so I smeared them with Rosebud. The dry crust rubbed off on my fingers, and I wiped it in the tin. I still carry that tin around with me. Whenever I go to put on lip balm, I just move my finger around that crust. It's funny, sometimes as I'm doing it I hear my mother say: 'Have you *completely* lost your mind?' I guess maybe I *have* a little bit, you know?

When I went back downstairs, Djoeke was there. 'How about I make a big pot of soup?' she asked. It might sound weird, but for the rest of the day I was only worried about one thing: that something would go wrong with that soup. I worried that all of a sudden Djoeke would have to leave, and no one would be there to finish making the soup. For some reason, that soup became *terribly* important to me.

I went out on the balcony and called everyone to tell them what had happened at 8.30 that morning, and in between each call I went downstairs to check on the soup. It was maddening, to be honest. And it also became increasingly complicated as more and more people arrived. At one point, even *Elias Welverloren* showed up.

Elias Welverloren officiates all the funerals of intellectual Jews in Oud-Zuid. He knew my mother well, and when he saw her upstairs he said, 'Dear God, she's so yellow.' Can you believe it? 'Dear God, she's so yellow.' What I wanted to say was that everything was all right, even I was all right, but could he please just go downstairs and keep an eye on the goddamn soup.

And then those men showed up. You know the ones I'm talking about – the Ravens, as my aunt called them; she was there too by then. They were wearing black suits that were just a little too big, and as soon as they walked in, they muttered, 'My sympathies.' I couldn't help but laugh because I'd never heard anyone say 'my sympathies' before, and all of a sudden there were two people saying it at once, and incredibly fast. What I really needed was to cry, but sometimes you need to cry so badly that all you can do is laugh.

'Funny, is it?' said Elias Welverloren, and then I couldn't stop laughing because I started thinking about him, and how the rest of us were going to go through this once, but he did it all the time, and that at some point he had to eat lunch. That's what I started thinking about: that at some point Elias Welverloren has to have lunch between jobs, and that he probably chooses something *different* for lunch every time. For some reason, I found stuff like that hilarious that day.

Then the Ravens marched up the stairs, one after the other. My brother and I had to *race* after them. When we got to my room, one of them stared at my mother in disbelief, and then looked back at my brother. He asked my brother if she'd died of some terrible disease. Daniel looked at me, and then back at the man, and said, 'No.' My brother's funny like that: sometimes he just likes to keep things short.

Then the Ravens grabbed hold of the sheet my mother was lying on, and on the count of three they lifted her off the bed and folded the sheet around her. Then we couldn't see her any more. All of a sudden, I panicked. I don't know why, but I *really* panicked. I thought, okay, that's enough. My mother was a very independent woman, you know? Suddenly, I wanted to shout, 'Guys, she can do this herself.' Then I realized that my dad wasn't even there, he was downstairs making coffee again.

Daniel called to him to come up, and what I remember is him standing in the doorway clasping his hands. Then he nodded, and the Ravens pulled the sheet back over her face. They had lowered it so he could see her. And I know it's stupid to bring this up now, but in that moment I thought to myself: how nice it must be to be a man. People actually *look* at you when you nod. I could have nodded in that room too, but if anybody had even noticed, they'd probably have assumed it was some kind of tic. That poor girl's *completely* lost her mind, they'd have thought.

Then they put my mother in a black bag, which was later loaded into a black car. It was still incredibly hot outside, and while we were loading her into the car a Hummer drove by. 'They could *at least* slow down in this neighbourhood,' my dad snapped. If we'd left my dad to his own devices that day, he probably would've murdered everyone on our street. There would've been no one left in Oud-Zuid the next day. And then they just closed the door, you know? I never saw her again.

I hurried back in to check on the soup. But you know what Djoeke said when I walked into the kitchen? She said that I should start thinking about an obituary. Because I'm so good with words. But that's just it – as soon as something happens, I'm not good with words at all. I spent hours at the computer, even though the obituary was only supposed to be a couple of sentences. Otherwise, you have to shell out even more for the thing.

Suddenly, I thought of *Blue Is the Warmest Colour*, and about that infinite tenderness. That's what I wanted to write: that we would feel an infinite tenderness for her. And somehow the thought of it calmed me, because I knew that nobody could ever carry that tenderness away in a black bag and then load it into a black car. Nobody would even think of something like that. So I wrote it down. But then I had to write another sentence.

Well, it turned into a small disaster. It was really important to my dad that I write something like we would never forget her. To be honest, that seemed too obvious to me. The only thing I ever forget is how much I paid at Albert Heijn. I never take the receipt either. But other than that, I remember pretty much everything. So it felt like a waste of a sentence, but I wrote it anyway.

In the hour that followed, I made a crucial error. You know what I did? I used the verb *herinneren*, or 'to remember'. Here's my second-to-last tip for you: never use the verb *herinneren* in a text that people are going to go through with a fine-tooth

172

comb. Civil war broke out in our house. No one knew for sure whether it was reflexive or not. It is reflexive, by the way, and if we'd been in a normal state of mind, we would've known that – but we weren't. We were all upset and decided to blame everything on reflexive verbs. In moments like that, people need a scapegoat, and for us it was Dutch grammar.

God knows how long I sat at that computer. My back started to ache as the discussion became more heated. My dad and my brother were on one side, and Djoeke and my aunt were on the other. I swear they could've strangled each other. And *when* I'd got it written, in the reflexive form, my brother was the only one left in the room. He laid his hand on my shoulder and whispered: 'That's the most remarkable comma in the history of the Dutch language.' He was referring to the sentence before it. I swear to God, if I could have scooped up all the commas in the world at that moment, I would have thrown them at my brother and let him lie there for a while – buried in the rubble.

That evening I went home and stared out the window for a long time. I thought: from here on it only gets worse. That's what I thought: people always say that from here on it only gets better, which means that for me it will only get worse. Which is why I didn't want the day to end. So I just stared out the window, and after a while I started to dance.

'You don't dance to the beat, you dance to the lyrics,' people used to say to me. And that's true, I guess. I *only* pay attention to the lyrics. I can't help it; I wasn't raised in a musical home. My brother dances like a penguin, you know? My brother dances like a penguin, and I dance like a polar bear – a very lyrics-oriented polar bear. It's pretty painful to watch, but I danced anyway. And there was only one song that I danced to: 'Ain't Got No, I Got Life' by Nina Simone. But I didn't listen to it to the end: I pressed rewind every time she sang, 'Why am I alive, anyway?' After that, she starts to put things into perspective.

In that moment, I had no desire to hear Nina Simone putting things into perspective. I just wanted her to sing: 'Ain't got no mother, ain't got no culture.' But then I started thinking about it, and I actually *do* have a culture. And that made me feel guilty again, because maybe Nina Simone really didn't have anything, and all I didn't have was a mother. Sometimes I get a little too into the lyrics.

'We should give her a call' – that was my first thought when I woke up the next morning. I felt so guilty that we were organizing all of this without her. My family is an absolute mess without her. My mother was the one in the family who could be trusted with the main dish, if you know what I mean. With everyone else in the family, you think, okay, you can make the salad, or maybe just the dressing. And they'd even forget to do *that*. They're all great people, I swear, but you can't help but think, you know, why don't you just focus on your respiration for a little while. That's the only thing that you can *really* trust them with, respiration.

That afternoon I went to the Nieuwe Ooster cemetery with my father to pick out a grave. Little tip for people who are going to pick out a grave: don't eat too much beforehand. The man who drove us around the cemetery said, 'Fasten your seatbelts.' He drove us across the cemetery recklessly, in a kind of golf cart. I held on to my father for dear life, and when I looked up I saw that his eyes were closed. I think he hoped we were being driven to the afterlife. And to be honest, that's exactly how it felt.

Once in a while, the man offered a bit of information. He'd say, 'Mayor Eberhard,' and point to the right. But we were going so fast that the stone was already out of sight. About a minute after Eberhard, he stopped, and we were able to get out. I went over to a bush to catch my breath. My dad just stayed in the cart, and after a while he finally opened his eyes. 'Don't worry, they can wait,' the man said, and I burst out laughing. Normally, I hate men who make jokes like that, but the week my mum died I couldn't get enough of them.

I know it sounds stupid, but the plot he showed us was actually quite *serene*. It was next to my grandmother. My father was silent for a long time, and then he said, 'No, they'll start fighting again.' My dad was going a little mad at this point, too. But for some reason, the man seemed to understand completely. He pointed to another plot, right behind the bush I was standing by. 'From there they can still bicker a little bit,' he said. Now that really made me laugh. I was ready to take the guy home with me. But my dad just sighed and nodded, and finally he asked how many people could fit in that grave.

'Feel free to lie down beside it, sir,' the man replied. All of a sudden, I couldn't laugh any more. Suddenly, I was just done. 'Do you bury people on Sundays?' my dad asked once we were back at the office. 'No, God help us,' the man replied. But we'd already scheduled my mother's funeral. She was to be buried on Monday. I didn't understand why my dad wanted to know that, and I didn't really want to. By then, I'd really had enough.

And you know whose birthday it was on Monday? Mine. It's ridiculous, really, but the funeral was on my birthday. That's actually how I wanted to start this book: 'On my twenty-fifth birthday, I buried my mother.' It seemed like a strong first sentence. Here's the opening paragraph I had in mind:

On my twenty-fifth birthday, I buried my mother. To be more precise, we lowered her down, at a pace that was not entirely even. Beforehand, the undertaker had told us that it was better not to let the rope glide through your hands, but to alternate your grip between your left and right hand. This would help to prevent blisters. In the end, everyone did it their own way, and my mother went down swinging. Later, I thought about it more and realized that it was something that took practice. Which is why it's a shame that death is such a one-time thing – I was only able to let go of my mother once.

God, what a strange day that was. People kept saying to me, 'Happy birthday, by the way.' I couldn't stand it. I hate it when people have to tag on a 'by the way'. What's it supposed to mean? That morning I got a text message from Rose: 'Happy bday & sry 4 yr loss.' Kind of a weird message when you think about it. But at least it's more specific than 'by the way'.

As we lowered my mother into the grave, I couldn't help but think back to my grandmother's funeral. It had been a year earlier, and my mother almost fell into the grave. She didn't let the rope glide through her hands, she just let it pull her down with it. My mum was very confused around that time, or that's how we described it. She was very confused, and eventually it got so bad that she would head off to Albert Heijn and not come back. She just couldn't make up her mind. So I started going with her sometimes, and I'd say, 'You pick out the vegetables.' She needed very precise instructions. After a while, I'd come back to the produce section, and she'd still be standing there with an empty basket. Just staring at all the lettuces.

That's when my mother left for the first time. When a person is very, very confused, it's like there's nobody there. You can still look at them, but there's no one home. It's horrible, to be honest. She kept asking me if I wanted a cookie. After a while you figure out that it doesn't matter what you say. Eventually, she'd come back and say, 'Darling, you're so thin.' But I wasn't very thin at all. Not any thinner than usual. *She* was thin. But she didn't think she deserved any cookies. That was the whole problem: my mum suddenly thought she didn't *deserve* anything any more.

While we were lowering her casket, Chiel played his horn. A lot of people cried as he played, but I didn't cry until he stopped. I cried because I saw him crying, and actually I only really started crying when I hugged him and smelled that he was wearing Lynx again. All of a sudden, it made me so sad, you know? Him, the Hilton Hotel, Dennis Bergkamp walking by without a word.

The next day was the memorial service, where there was no Mahler played. That was very important to my father. 'No Mahler, people will start crying.' Instead, someone sang 'You Don't Know What Love Is' by Ella Fitzgerald, and I don't know how many people cried because I was sitting way at the front. I was sitting way at the front, where the people who are grieving the most are supposed to sit. I thought about that later too, and I realized that there's a difference. A difference between the saddest people and the people with the most *right* to be sad. Of the two, only the latter can actually be calculated and taken into consideration, and nobody ever asked me how sad I actually was.

If they had asked, I probably wouldn't have been able to answer. Come to think of it, I was actually pretty happy at my mother's memorial service. People were finally paying attention for once, you know? That's all I've ever really wanted – for people to pay attention. It's the only way to not be alone.

And we were together. Jules was there, with her strong, clear-cut face, and a few chairs down was Frida, with Lotti and Lola on either side. I thought of Lola's thesis, and wondered whether she had finished it yet. Jennifer was there too, and so was Kyra, and I wondered if she still made gigantic leeks that had to be strapped to the roof of a car even though they didn't add anything to the storyline.

All of a sudden, I wanted to say, 'Please don't ever stop making leeks, and don't let anyone ever finish their thesis.' In fact, I wanted to make some kind of decree that no one should ever get out of their chair again. That's what I hoped for: that everyone would go on sitting right where they were.

And I still don't know how sad I actually am. Honestly, I have no idea. After that summer, they gave me a bunch of pills. I got this ringing in my ear, and it still hasn't gone away. It sounds kind of like a siren. Normally a siren comes closer and then fades, but this siren just stays. It's enough to drive a person crazy. But the funny thing is that you were already crazy, and that's why your ear started ringing in the first place. Sometimes that's exactly what I want to say to my lively, intense mind: 'Guys, it's already mad enough in here.' But sometimes your mind doesn't listen.

'It numbs everything a bit,' the doctor said. And she wasn't kidding. If you take enough of those pills, after a while all you know is your own name. With everything else, you just think – whatever. Occasionally a little voice will ask, 'Is it really "whatever" though?' And then a loud, booming voice will waltz in and say, 'Of course it is.' It's like a bar conversation between two people who've run out of things to talk about.

Actually, the ringing was there before my mother died. It had started about a year earlier, when I decided to tell my parents all the things I've already told you about. About girls and sex, and about how all I can ever think of to say is that the *bartender* thinks they're the prettiest girl in De Trut, because that's the only thing I know for sure. That's what I wanted to tell them: that there's so little I know for sure, that I've always been wrong – wrong about the boys and wrong about the girls, and that I wanted to make an appointment at the VU Medical

Center, where you can become less of a girl and more of a boy. That's how I like to put it, you know? *More* boy. Boys themselves are really pretty pathetic. But just – a little more boy.

You know what my parents did? They pretended I never said anything. Sometimes parents are really terrible people. They like to think of you as this finished product. So when you mention the VU Medical Center, they don't want to hear it. And that's when the ringing started. They did send me to an ear specialist, by the way. In that sense, they were incredibly accommodating. Then my dad started talking about what's covered by insurance and what's not.

The ear doctor asked me about my stress triggers, and don't ask me why, but I replied, 'I'm a lesbian.' Sometimes I hope that that alone says it all. But it never does, so I added, 'And I have a book deal.' Well, that piqued his interest. It's weird, but whenever you tell people you have a book deal, they bring up talk shows. They don't even ask what your book is about, you know? If he'd asked, I could've said, 'My stress triggers.'

But the doctor just started going on about his favourite talk show host and said that one day I'd be sitting next to him. Afterwards, he said, 'There's nothing wrong with your ears. It's in your head.' And that's how, slowly but surely, those pills became part of my life. They're the same pills my mother took when she couldn't make up her mind in the produce section, which bothers me sometimes. But then I just pop another one until all I can think is: whatever.

Pretty silly, isn't it? How it all turned out? Sometimes I think about my mother, but then I wonder, where did she go? That's the whole point: I don't miss my mother – I don't understand where she is. It would be really nice if you could tell me. You've been awfully quiet this whole time. And that's the crazy thing – *everybody* has become so quiet. Maybe they're afraid I'll start crying, and I get that.

Though there is one person who brings it up every now and then: my boss at the pizzeria where I work. I make pizzas now. She just asks me stuff. About what my mother was like and how we got along. 'I'm just so *curious*, Sof, so *curious*,' she says. She's not the least bit afraid that I'll start crying. And that, of all things, makes me want to cry. Not for my mother, but because there is someone who dares to get close. There's something incredibly sweet about people who dare to get close. *Sweethearts*, that's what they are.

One time she asked if my mother left me with any life lessons that have stayed with me. I replied that my mother had better things to do than throw one-liners at me all the time. I can be really short with people, but that's just because I need to focus on the pizzas. They're like those onions in Hot Dog Bush – whatever you do, don't let them burn.

But on the way home, I thought about it again. I was on the ferry, you know, because the job is in Amsterdam-Noord. So I was on the ferry, leaning against the wall, and suddenly I remembered: 'Never ride through red lights on Wibautstraat.' That's what my mother taught me, you know? 'You can ride through red anywhere else, but not on Wibautstraat.' I couldn't help but smile at the thought. Because you know what's funny? I *always* do.

Keep in touch with
Granta Books:

Visit granta.com to discover more.

GRANTA